Meet Alex O'Connell. He's twelve years old and loves the world he's discovered living in Egypt in 1937. More than anything, Alex wants to be a Medjai. He's learned that Medjai must work to keep dark forces locked inside mummies' tombs where they belong. First, Alex must prove himself worthy of becoming a Medjai. How hard could it be? He doesn't expect the Scorpion King, the fiercest creature of the underworld, to rise from the dead in search of revenge!

To make matters worse, if German soldiers sacrifice a living soul, the Scorpion King will let them rule the world for a thousand years. Will Alex be able to stop this dangerous deal—before it's too late?

JUN 5 2001

BOOK I

REVENGE OF THE SCORPION KING

by Dave Wolverton

Based on the motion picture screenplay
The Mummy Returns by Stephen Sommers

BANTAM BOOKS

NEW YORK • TORONTO • LONDON • SYDNEY • AUCKLAND

MANHATTAN PUBLIC LIBRARY DIST

RL 5.0 AGES 009-012

REVENGE OF THE SCORPION KING

A Bantam Skylark Book / April 2001

Copyright © 2001 Universal Studios Publishing Rights, a division of Universal Studios Licensing, Inc. THE MUMMY and THE MUMMY RETURNS are trademarks and copyrights of Universal Studios. All rights reserved.
Cover art copyright © 2001 by Cliff Nielsen with photograph of The Rock courtesy of Universal Studios.

A Note to Parents: The film *The Mummy Returns* is rated PG-13.
Consult www.filmratings.com for further information.

All rights reserved. No part of this book may be reproduced or transmitted in any form or by any means, electronic or mechanical, including photocopying, recording, or by any information storage and retrieval system, without permission in writing from the publisher. For information address Bantam Books.

If you purchased this book without a cover you should be aware that this book is stolen property. It was reported as "unsold and destroyed" to the publisher and neither the author nor the publisher has received any payment for this "stripped book."

ISBN: 0-553-48754-X

Visit us on the Web! www.randomhouse.com/kids

Educators and librarians, for a variety of teaching tools, visit us at www.randomhouse.com/teachers

Published simultaneously in the United States and Canada

BANTAM SKYLARK is an imprint of Random House Children's Books, a division of Random House, Inc. SKYLARK BOOK and colophon and BANTAM BOOKS and colophon are registered trademarks of Random House, Inc. Bantam Books, 1540 Broadway, New York, New York 10036.

PRINTED IN THE UNITED STATES OF AMERICA

OPM 10 9 8 7 6 5 4 3 2 1

3 8001 00044 0366

CONTENTS

Prologue
THE SCORPION KING AWAKES

VALLEY OF AHM SHERE, EGYPT—1937

In the shadowy Temple of Anubis, green mold and yellow fungus spotted the golden walls. Hieroglyphs etched into the stone wavered in torchlight. Mummies lined the far wall, filling the temple with the smell of decaying bodies.

And the Scorpion King rose from the dead in agony.

Thousands of black scorpions were stinging him, their tails piercing his muscular chest like fiery needles. He was part man, part scorpion, and the rigid scales on his six legs and giant tail were swarming with deadly creatures. The scorpion's venom surged into him, hotter and more potent than blood.

The Scorpion King stared at the Spear of Osiris wedged in his chest, the cold tip piercing his heart.

Four years ago, the Scorpion King had risen from a six-thousand-year slumber to conquer the earth with his master's army. If it hadn't been for Rick O'Connell, he would have succeeded. Instead, O'Connell had heaved the deadly spear into the Scorpion King's chest, making him explode into a sea of black vapor. Never to be heard from again. Until now.

As his surprise at waking to life was swallowed in the agony of scorpion stings, the Scorpion King roared. Before him, a lord of the Anubis warriors held a torch of flickering flame. The Anubis lord was a terrifying creature, with the warped body of a man and a grizzly canine head.

Yet the Anubis warrior was not as horrifying as the Scorpion King, with the bare bones of his skull exposed and his giant black scorpion's body.

"A gift for you," a voice growled. It was not the voice of the Anubis warrior, nor was it human. The words seemed to flutter through the air like bats, while the sound seeped from the dirt floor as if from a grave. It was Anubis himself, the jackal-headed Egyptian god of the dead.

"When I helped you defeat your enemies six thousand years ago, you sold me your soul," Anubis whispered. "You promised to serve me forever. Four years ago, you failed me. I will not release you from that bargain, even for such a small thing as death."

"Anubis takes life, Anubis gives life. Great are the gifts of Anubis," the Scorpion King intoned. A leering grin split his face as he raised a pincer and then closed it with enough force to snap an iron bar. He grasped the Spear of Osiris in his chest and yanked it out with a groan. The wound oozed black blood and venom, then mended. Years of healing took place in moments. The Scorpion King rose on his six feet.

"Now, I have a task for you," Anubis hissed. "When O'Connell destroyed you, his brother-in-law stole the diamond from the crown of my pyramid. Powerful men have retrieved it. Find out what they want—and bring me back my jewel."

For ages, the Scorpion King had guarded Anubis's temple at Ahm Shere. Many men had sought to enter. None had made it out alive. Except for the O'Connells.

Fire surged through the Scorpion King's veins. "I shall restore the diamond, my lord, and avenge the honor of your temple," the Scorpion King swore.

Anubis roared in delight, then stopped abruptly.

A silence fell over the dim temple. "There is a boy who will try to stand in your way," he whispered. "O' Connell's son . . . Alex. Stop him."

The Scorpion King scowled. This time, there would be no mercy. "Arise, my warriors!" he shouted to the mummies that lined the wall. "Shake the dust from your bones. Death to the infidels!"

1
BAD-LUCK ALEX

EGYPTIAN DESERT, SOUTH OF ASWAN—1937

As he ran, Alex O'Connell tried again to shake the Bracelet of Anubis from his wrist. Still locked tight. Behind him he could hear the bones of the fierce pygmy skeletons pounding against the ground as they chased him and his father through the jungle of Ahm Shere. If Alex and his father didn't get to the golden pyramid of Anubis before the sun hit it, the bracelet was going to destroy him . . . and if they didn't outrun the pygmies, they would be devoured.

"Now that the bracelet is on Alex's wrist," Ardeth Bay had warned, "the Scorpion King will wake and raise the Army of Anubis." Ardeth Bay was their trusted friend and the leader of the Medjai. For five thousand years, these bold adventurers had guarded mummies' tombs, trying to keep foolish men from unleashing the evil locked inside.

"We must kill the Scorpion King and send his warriors back to the underworld. Otherwise"—Ardeth Bay had paused—"the Scorpion King will wipe out the world." Only

this time, Ardeth Bay's warning had come too late. The O'Connells had stumbled into a disaster.

Alex and his father dove into the temple's entrance just as the sun struck the top of the golden pyramid. Pop! The bracelet opened and clattered to the floor.

Suddenly, the ground began to shake and tremble. "Who disturbs the Temple of Anubis?" a voice bellowed from the hall, as thundering footsteps headed their way.

Alex and his father stared at each other in horror, remembering Ardeth Bay's words.

The footsteps grew louder, as Alex prepared to die. . . .

Alex O'Connell woke with a start, his heart beating loudly in his chest. He looked quickly around, then breathed a sigh of relief. It was only a dream, the same one he'd had since meeting the Scorpion King four years ago. He was in the desert, and the Scorpion King was dead.

By the light of ten thousand stars, a huge black scorpion stalked through the dirt toward his hand.

Just what I need now, Alex thought, *bugs trying to poison me.* Nervous sweat trickled down his face.

He hated scorpions, but he didn't move. For hours he had been spying on a camp of men that he suspected were tomb raiders. But the afternoon sun had lulled him to sleep. Now a German guard stood ten feet away, a machine gun cradled in his arm. Fifty yards away, a group of men sprawled around several campfires. Half a dozen of them were guards. Alex hardly dared breathe, much less creep away from the scorpion.

If Alex was caught, the men might think he was a thief. By Egyptian law, they could chop off his hands for stealing. These Germans looked like a grim bunch. They might just shoot him.

Alex remained perfectly still, hidden in a cluster of rocks. He crouched on hands and knees with his back bent and his head down so that his tan robes looked like a rock. Pebbles cut into his palms and knees. A black turban covered his head.

Alex suspected that the robes and darkness could not hide him. The campfires were too bright, and a couple of tents had lamps lit inside, so they glowed like coals.

The scorpion scampered forward and stopped mere inches from his hand.

Alex tried to calm himself. He centered his mind on the teachings of Ardeth Bay, whispering, "The

Medjai protect mankind in secret, not openly. The Medjai should see, but not be seen. The Medjai should strike, and no cry should ever be raised."

The Medjai should not fall asleep on duty, he added, blushing.

More than anything, twelve-year-old Alex wanted to be a Medjai, a guardian of the mummies' tombs. He had seen the powerful forces hidden in these tombs firsthand and didn't want tomb raiders to make the same mistake he'd made. The risk was too great.

He'd been studying the ways of the Medjai every chance he had since meeting his parent's friend, Ardeth Bay, four years ago. Now when Alex's parents were away, they often left him with Ardeth Bay. The Lord of the Medjai was a trustworthy man.

Ardeth Bay's idea of child rearing was nothing like Alex's mum's. For her, education meant studying Latin and ancient Egyptian. Ardeth Bay agreed—except he included sword fighting in the daily lessons. If Alex was to be a Medjai, he had to know how to sabotage tomb raiders' efforts.

Even after four years of studying the ways of the Medjai, Alex had not yet become one of them.

Knowing how to swing a sword didn't make a man a Medjai. He had to prove that he was a "true protector of mankind," with perfect courage and tenacity.

That's why Alex was in this situation now. His mum and dad had left by ship for England, where his mum would be presenting a paper to the Bembridge scholars. They would be there for three weeks.

During this time Ardeth Bay had decided that Alex was ready for his *Mushwâr Wa*, his lone walk. Alex could begin to prove that he was worthy to become a Medjai. He had no idea where Ardeth Bay and the other Medjai might be. But this morning Alex had spotted some suspicious-looking Germans leaving the town of Aswan. As a Medjai in training, it was Alex's duty to follow their caravan and spy on them. If they were just honest folks, he'd leave them alone. But if they were tomb raiders . . .

In the distance Alex heard an engine growl as a car moved over the desert. Three yards away, a cricket chirped.

Alex bit his lip as the scorpion crawled closer. It hesitated only an inch from his hand. Perhaps the scorpion thought his finger was a cricket.

Alex's eyes shifted back up to the guard. The big

man stared over Alex's head at the empty desert and drew a long puff on a cigarette.

Alex wondered why the Germans needed so many guards. *Maybe they're just scaredy-cats.*

The guard overhead tossed his cigarette on the ground and strode back to the campfire.

The scorpion raised its tail and lurched forward. Alex slammed his fist on the insect before it could deliver a killing sting. "Dreadfully sorry!" Alex whispered.

Then he peered up. No one was watching. He sneaked from the rocks to a shadow beneath a nearby truck. He wanted to find out what kind of equipment the Germans were carrying.

The Germans had some Egyptian servants in their camp. The servants, the *suffragis,* were roasting pigeons over the campfire. The spicy scent made Alex's mouth water as he neared the truck. From a nearby tent, he could smell pipe smoke. But beneath these sweet aromas, he detected another that he knew too well—the dusty odor of rotted mummies.

The Germans have already found a tomb! That's why the guards are so edgy. The trucks might be full of mummies and gold.

If they were all lucky, no one would get hurt. Powerful spells guarded the tombs.

This settled it. Alex felt he couldn't just spy on the Germans anymore; he had to take action. For thousands of years, the Medjai had believed and told others that bad luck followed anyone who tried to rob the tombs.

"Well," Alex muttered, "tonight my name is 'Bad Luck,' and I'm about to strike hard."

The tomb raiders had three supply trucks, and a hundred camels and horses were bedded down on the far side of camp. Alex settled on his plan: wreck the trucks and scare off the animals. The Germans would have no choice but to crawl back to Cairo.

Distantly, Alex heard the car again, then saw its headlights bouncing along a far-off trail. He imagined the car pulling up to the trucks, pinning him with its beams. He would have to hurry to get out.

Alex slid into the shadows between two of the large trucks. Each truck had a canvas top on it. Oil drums were stacked nearby in a small pyramid. Alex figured that the oil drums would help shield him from prying eyes. He scooped up a handful of sand that was still warm from the blistering heat of the day. He crept to the gas tank of the nearest truck and began to take off the gas cap. The tin cap made a small grinding sound as he twisted.

He stopped. It wasn't a loud sound, but the Medjai were supposed to work in total silence.

No one was close. Alex pulled it off quickly and tossed some sand into the gas tank. The sand would ruin the engine. The truck would never make it another mile on the road.

One truck down, two to go.

Alex was just putting the gas cap back on when he felt the truck jiggle. *Oh no,* he thought. *There are guards in the truck!*

He rolled beneath the truck. As he lay on the warm sand, he saw a pair of feet drop softly to the ground by the rear bumper. Someone crouched for half a second.

Alex's heart pounded.

The Germans are after me!

2

FOOT ROT AND DYNAMITE

Quicker than a lizard, Alex scurried out and crawled beneath the next truck over. He watched his pursuer creep around the side of the first truck and glance beneath it.

Alex scooted behind a tire. Someone was definitely on to him. Every instinct screamed for him to run. But the words of Ardeth Bay came to mind: "A man who does not rule his fear will become a slave to it."

Better a live slave than a corpse! Alex thought. He rolled beneath the third truck. With the shadows of the trucks as his only cover, he raced twenty yards and threw himself behind a rock.

He sat for three seconds, terrified that he had been spotted. He glanced back.

His pursuer had moved to the second truck—still searching, still listening.

Alex dared not move. He gritted his teeth. A German military staff car, a ragtop convertible with the top down, entered camp. Alex expected it to pull even with the other trucks. But instead it wheeled right next to the campfires. In the back seat was a German army officer—a *Kommandant*—who sat with stiff formality in a crisp uniform. He looked like a cruel, brutish man.

The tomb raiders leapt to their feet, barking "*Heil Hitler!*" There was an edge of fear to their voices.

From one glowing tent, the tomb raiders' leader emerged. In his hand was a black walking stick carved from ebony, a silver dog's head at its top. He was a tall man in fine clothes, but he looked so thin that he seemed to be a walking skeleton.

Then Alex saw a sight that made his mouth go dry. A small figure limped behind the leader—the corpse of a rotting pygmy!

The corpse was not a mummy, for it was not wrapped in bandages. Instead, the ghoul wore the remains of some spoiled furs. Half of its face was torn away, revealing the naked roots of filed teeth. It carried a crude spear in one hand, and it wore a rubbery shrunken monkey's paw as a necklace. Parts of its feet had rotted away, so it walked in a horrid, shambling gait. It hissed and slavered.

The horrible sound sent shivers down Alex's spine. All thoughts of his pursuer were driven from his mind. He'd only seen a ghoul like this—this Foot Rot creature—once before, at the tomb of the Scorpion King. He'd never seen such a monster tag along behind a living man. *Why is it following him?*

Behind the ghoul, a large mummy soldier followed, bearing an ancient brass sword.

"Wilkommen, Kommandant R.," the skeletal leader of the tomb raiders called. He planted his black staff in the ground and bowed slightly, a fawning gesture.

The commandant nodded in return, dismissing the man with an air of contempt. He focused on the ghoul and asked a brusque question. The skeletal tomb raider began translating into ancient Egyptian, *"Neb Commandant R. åpå ur hesi tua . . ."* Alex had learned enough ancient Egyptian from his mother that he could follow the conversation. "Kommandant R. finds you to be most fascinating. . . . But he wonders if it is wise to rely on such a devil."

Alex had never heard a corpse speak before, but

when the little ghoul began to hiss, Alex found he could somehow make out its answer, "This 'devil' can be trusted—so long as your lord keeps *his* end of the bargain."

Commandant R. was a big man with a steely gaze. He eyed the ghoul with distaste. Yet he held up a satchel, as if to offer proof that he would keep some demonic bargain.

Foot Rot rubbed its hands together like a greedy merchant in the bazaar and hissed, "Excellent! Most excellent! My master will be pleased."

The tomb raider nodded. "You will take us to the location. And Hitler will reward me properly."

Alex suddenly realized that he'd gotten distracted. He glanced back toward the trucks but couldn't see the guard who had been hunting for him. The leader of the tomb raiders and the ghoul climbed into the front of the staff car, and Commandant R. sat in back. The silent soldier mummy stayed behind.

Where are they going? Alex wondered. He tried to remember a spell that Ardeth Bay had taught him. The spell was supposed to put mummies to sleep. Alex knew it was risky. He recalled Ardeth Bay's warning. "This spell will work on most mummies, if Allah is willing. Some mummies cannot resist it. The old kings made most of their mummies from slaves. They even made mummies of cats, monkeys, owls, and bulls. This spell will put all such mortal creatures to sleep.

"But there are other mummies created by powerful wizards—" Ardeth Bay had shuddered, his eyes hardening. "Beware of them!"

It was a simple spell. Alex knew the translation: *In the presence of Horus of the Two Eyes, I command you to sleep in your eternal tomb.*

Alex was supposed to say it in ancient Egyptian. He focused his gaze on the soldier mummy and whispered, *"_Heru-ur-khenti-år-ti, aa_m . . . gab ås-t . . . ?"* He couldn't remember the last word. *Har? . . . Heem? What* was it? He wished that he had his Budge's *Dictionary of Ancient Egyptian* handy.

But suddenly the mummy dropped its sword, put its hand to its mouth, yawned, and then stood there looking stupid.

Well, Alex thought, *it's half asleep. Maybe the spell takes a little time.*

Alex focused on the soldier mummy again and whispered, "*_Heru-ur-khenti-år-ti, aa_m qab ås-t . . . heb?*"

The soldier mummy snapped to attention and lowered its head as if it were a charging bull. It spun and ran straight at the closest truck. *Thud!* It slammed into the driver's door and leaned against the truck, moaning.

Alex ducked his head. "*That's not supposed to happen!*"

A huge *boom* shook the camp. Fire shot through the sky as oil drums by the truck began exploding. The drums hurtled into the air like rockets. Germans began screaming, "*Wasser!*" Water!

Men were diving for cover. On the far side of camp, horses bucked and pulled down their tie lines. Camels fought at their hobbles, and servants began rushing about, trying to calm the terrified animals. The blast had knocked one truck to its side. All three trucks were on fire.

Suddenly, one of the trucks exploded, hurling debris into the air.

Hot wind roared over Alex as a burning oil drum

crashed on a tent, splashing oil all about. The tent quickly burst into flames.

"Ooof!" Alex cried, as a piece of rotten flesh landed on him. The soldier mummy was on fire! As its bandages burned, it clawed at the flames like some wounded animal. Scarab beetles raced out of its silently screaming mouth.

Alex poured some water from his canteen onto the flames, and the mummy went still, never to move again. Alex shoved it aside. Lifting its dry body was like picking up a big pillow.

Suddenly, he heard footsteps rushing toward him. "The ghoul!" he whispered, almost blind with panic. "Or a German guard!"

Someone came leaping behind the rock, almost on top of him. Alex clenched his hand into a fist and prepared to swing. But in the light of the explosions, Alex caught a glimpse of the person. Thankfully, it wasn't a mummy or a guard—it was an Egyptian girl, not more than thirteen years old. She wore a simple brown robe, with a shawl wrapped around her head. She crouched behind the rock and pulled a stick of dynamite from her pocket.

She had blown up the oil drums!

The girl focused on the Germans and prepared to creep away. As she did, her hand accidentally touched Alex's face. She stiffened in terror.

"Are you going to pick my nose or just hold it?" Alex whispered.

She gasped.

"Quiet!" Alex slapped his hand over her mouth. "I'm a friend."

"If you don't talk softer," she shot back, "you'll be a corpse."

But the warning came too late.

"Ein Saboteur!" someone cried. The girl stared at him, eyes wide in panic.

Three guards were rushing toward them. A burst of machine-gun fire opened up. Sparks flew as bullets bounced off the rocks around them.

"We have to get out of here!" Alex cried. The ground rocked as the gas tank on a truck exploded. The girl grabbed Alex's hand and jerked hard. They ran toward an outcropping of rock. Gunfire erupted from camp. Bullets slammed into the ground at their feet. Suddenly she pulled him behind some rocks.

They couldn't stay long. The girl held up her

stick of dynamite. "This is my last." She kissed it for luck and lobbed it toward the camp. It landed in back of a burning truck. The guards saw the dynamite and dropped for cover. The truck exploded, sending supplies hurtling everywhere.

"Come on!" Alex said, grabbing her wrist and leading her toward his camel. They raced down the rocky bed of a dry stream, around a bend, then up a low hill covered in boulders.

No gunfire followed for several minutes, and Alex realized that they might make it out of there alive. A guard in Commandant R.'s car began flashing a spotlight over the hills as his men searched for them. Alex and the girl did not stop until they reached a hill nearly a mile away.

Alex's camel was hobbled just beyond the rise.

He rested amid some huge boulders, gasping for breath. Sweat rolled down his forehead. The girl crouched beside him, watching the camp, admiring her handiwork. The fires still raged in the trucks, and light reflected from the oily smoke.

Everywhere the camp was in disarray. Men chased camels and horses and tried to put out the fires by smothering them with sand. The oil drums and trucks had been parked on the outskirts of camp. No one had been hurt or killed. But the Germans were as mad as wasps.

Alex wondered what the tomb raiders were up to. What were they doing with a ghoul and a German commander? Whatever it was, it couldn't be good.

I should warn Ardeth Bay, he thought. *But not yet. Not until I know what we're up against.*

Alex pulled off his turban and began to wind it more tightly around his head. "Couldn't you have found a less spectacular way to ruin the trucks?" he asked.

The girl pushed strands of black hair under her shawl and didn't answer.

"Why would you bomb the camp? Someone could have been killed."

"No one could have been killed," the girl said fiercely, her brown eyes blazing. "I did not set the bombs near people."

Her English was perfect, but Alex detected an accent. She was German.

"But—you're German!"

"Not like them. I'm a Jew. Since Hitler came to power in Germany, he took away our citizenship.

Now his men burn our homes, our books, and smash our stores. We are at war."

"We?" Alex asked. His parents had told him about the tensions in Germany, but he had not heard that war had broken out.

"*Them* and *me*," she explained.

"Then I'm lucky I'm not one of them," Alex said with a grin. He finished wrapping his turban and fastened it with its gold pin. Beside him, the girl wiped dirt from her face with the back of her hand, then tightened her worn leather sandals.

Where are her parents? Alex wondered, glancing quickly downhill. Light glinted off a gun as a guard searched the rocks a hundred yards below. There was no more time for small talk. "So, soldier," he whispered, "are you bulletproof, or do you just act that way?"

"My name is Rachel Stroeker—and I try to be."

"Well, Rachel, unless you're more bulletproof than I, Alex O'Connell, am, I think we should get out of here. My camel can carry us both." He took her hand and raced uphill.

3

MYSTERIES REVEALED

As they reached Alex's camel, Rachel took one whiff and held her nose. "Ugh!"

"What's the matter?" Alex asked. "Don't you like Stinkwad? He might not smell like much, but he's the fastest camel in the desert."

"That's because all of the other camels try to chase him away, I'll bet," Rachel said. "Do you have any water?"

"Water? Sure." Alex got his canteen and swished it. Less than half full. He gave the camel some in his palm.

"Is my English so bad?" Rachel asked. "*I* wanted the water."

"It's the custom here in the desert," Alex said. "You always give the camel a drink before you take one yourself. Otherwise, Stinkwad here will get mad, and then he'll just sit while the Germans use us for target practice."

"Oh," Rachel said, miffed. He finished watering Stinkwad, then gave a drink to Rachel. She gulped greedily, as if she hadn't had a drink in days.

Alex took off the camel's hobbles, put them in the saddlebags, and saddled the camel. They climbed on together, Alex in front, Rachel holding him lightly by the waist from behind.

He used a prod to get Stinkwad to his feet and urged the camel out across the sand. The moon was beginning to rise, a dark red moon that colored the whole landscape. A cool night breeze blew. With luck, the wind would blow away the camel's tracks by dawn.

Something bothered Alex. He thought about what he'd seen. Obviously, the leader of the tomb raiders was setting up a trade between the ghoul and Commandant R., but Alex had never heard of anyone making deals with the dead. Who was the ghoul's leader, what did it want, and what would the Germans gain in return?

"Can you drop me off in Aswan?" Rachel asked.

It was the nearest town, only a day away. Alex had followed the German caravan out from Aswan this morning. Rachel must have stayed hidden in the back of the truck all day, until she felt it was time to strike.

"Is that where you live?" Alex asked.

"No, Cairo. My father works in the embassy there. But I can take the train home from Aswan."

"Hmmm . . . Aswan," Alex said thoughtfully. "Sure, I'll drop you off. But first you have to pay."

"Pay?" she said. "I . . . I don't have any extra money."

"Okay," he said, "then we'll barter. I'll give you a ride, but you answer my questions. For example, do you have any idea who the Germans are or what they are up to?"

"I don't know much," Rachel replied. "I think the man who runs the camp is named Zorin Ungricht."

"Ungricht!" Alex cried. "My dad warned me about him. Ungricht hunts for treasure, and if you get in his way, he'll kill you! He nearly killed my dad in a temple in India. Ungricht will do *anything* for money. What about the commandant?"

"Commandant R. is a friend to Hitler. He was

bringing a bribe to pay to someone, a criminal I think. They kept talking about the ghoul's leader, *der König der Skorpions*, the 'King of Scorpions.' "

Alex pulled Stinkwad's reins, halting the camel abruptly. In anger, the beast turned its head and spit.

It can't be! Alex had seen his father kill the Scorpion King four years ago. *If the Scorpion King is alive, then*—Alex shuddered at the memory—*Anubis warriors can't be far behind.*

"I know where they're going," Alex said. "If we hurry through the hills, we can beat them." He turned the camel and began to race south.

Rachel stiffened. "You said you'd take me to Aswan. Are you a thief, Alex? Is that why you were at the camp—to steal the bribe money?"

Alex laughed. "No. I was there to sabotage the trucks, like you. But I prefer to do it quietly."

"Why?" Rachel asked.

"Because if you sneak in and sneak out, there's a better chance that you can get away alive."

"No," Rachel said, "I meant, why did you want to wreck their trucks in the first place?"

"Those men are tomb raiders," Alex explained.

"But more than gold hides in the mummies' tombs. There are books of magic spells—and mummies that know how to use them. The ancient kings of Egypt hired guards to keep people from unleashing the powers locked in those tombs. For thousands of years, the guards have done their job. They are called the Medjai, and my friend is their leader. Now, I'm training to become one of them."

"And?" Rachel stared at him, unconvinced.

"*And* the Scorpion King is the most powerful creature of all. When he rose four years ago, he and his warriors nearly destroyed my whole family. If the Germans make a deal with him . . . there's no telling what they'll be able to do."

Rachel dug her heels into Stinkwad. "Then Aswan can wait," she replied. "Lead the way!"

When Alex told Rachel that Stinkwad was the fastest camel in the desert, he wasn't lying—by much. "Hyah!" he called. The camel raced off.

4
A DEADLY DEAL

Near dawn, Alex and Rachel hobbled Stinkwad and climbed a ridge that looked over the moonlit valley of Ahm Shere. The golden pyramid was gone, just as Alex had hoped. Four years ago, it had been out there half a mile away, but when Alex's father killed the Scorpion King, the whole pyramid and the surrounding oasis had sunk beneath the earth. Alex exhaled. *Then there is still time.*

The Germans' car droned in the distance, its headlights casting eerie shadows on the stony valley. In front of the ridge where Alex hid, a line of statues had been carved from sandstone—statues of the jackal-headed god Anubis. Each statue was a hundred feet tall. Their feet touched the valley below, and their heads rose even with the ridge top. They stood like guardians to the west of the old temple site, gazing east with vacant eyes. Each statue held a scepter shaped like an *ankh*, a cross with a loop at its top, the Egyptian symbol of eternal life. Over the ages, windblown sand had worn away the statues' faces and made hollows in their eyes. Still, they seemed as constant and majestic as the stars.

Alex led Rachel to a spot behind the shoulder of a statue and sat to wait for the Germans. He felt as if he hadn't just traveled over land, but had traveled back in time.

Whenever Alex visited Egypt with his parents, he felt the same way. Egypt in all of its splendor and beauty was his passion. These feelings of awe were the reason he wanted to be a Medjai.

The first time he had seen the ancient Sphinx, he was only three. After his parents had finished exploring the pyramids of Giza, they had taken Alex to see the great statue. They had even had a picnic beneath the lion, and he had gazed up at the Sphinx's head, which had the face of a pharaoh with its royal headdress and beard.

Abu el Hol, "the Father of Terror," the Sphinx was called in Arabic. The statue had not filled him with terror. It filled him with wonder at its sheer size and beauty. He felt sad that it was being eroded over time. One of the seven great wonders of the world was hurt. Even at three years old, Alex had wanted to save it all. He still felt that way now.

He glanced at Rachel. "How long have you been in Egypt?"

"A week," Rachel answered. "But I learned Arabic years ago. When we fled Germany, my father joined the legion. We were stationed in Algeria first."

"Ah," Alex said. The French Foreign Legion had its headquarters in Algeria, in the city of Sidi Bel Abbès. "Has your father always been a soldier of fortune?"

"Not always," Rachel answered. "He detests men who kill only for money. He was a real soldier once. But there was no future for us in Germany."

"There's not much future in fighting your own war, either," Alex said. "What does your dad think about you doing this kind of thing?"

"He doesn't know," Rachel replied. "He is off on assignment. He thinks I spend the day at the French embassy in Cairo, combing the hair of my dolls."

Alex nodded. His own parents would be shocked to learn that he was out in the desert sabotaging the camps of tomb raiders.

Below, the car suddenly stopped. The driver turned off the headlights. The droning engine fell quiet, and the silence around Alex and Rachel seemed overwhelming, the wilderness endless.

"What do you think they're doing?" Rachel asked.

Alex pulled out his binoculars. He could see the men in the light of early dawn. Zorin Ungricht sat in the driver's seat, with Foot Rot beside him. Commandant R. sat in back. "They're waiting for something—or someone."

He scanned the countryside, but no one was near.

They waited until the rim of the sun crested the distant hills. Suddenly, Alex became aware of a soft hissing, as if sand were blowing across the desert. Yet in the past few hours, the winds had grown still. The hair rose on his head.

A black tide was rising, a tide of small bodies with feet that whispered in the sand as they shook and rose from the ground. Scorpions—millions of them—crawled up out of the rocks and swarmed around the Germans' car.

The car started slowly forward, casting an enormous shadow. The scorpions followed in a black wave, their tiny feet hissing through the sand, clicking against stones. Their poisonous stingers were curled above their backs. Alex imagined that if all the poison in those scorpions were poured out upon the sand, it would make a lake deep enough to drown in.

It was an odd procession. The car drove no faster than a scorpion could crawl.

Alex's mouth suddenly went dry. They were heading straight toward the old temple site! "Stay here and don't take your eyes off of them," he told Rachel. "I want to see if I can find a place to get a closer look."

"Closer? To a million scorpions?" Rachel asked. "Be my guest!"

Alex climbed down through the rocks, trying to find a path to the valley floor.

He had not gone a hundred yards when a cobra rose up from between two boulders. It spread its hood and gazed at him, tongue flickering.

Alex raised his palm and whispered a soothing greeting for cobras in ancient Egyptian, *"Mer-segrit."* The cobra seemed confused for a moment and then ducked its head and slithered back into the rocks.

"Yes!" he chuckled. "Works every time."

The car drew to a stop in the center of the valley, less than a quarter of a mile away. Alex raced down to some rocks, then raised his binoculars. Commandant R. stood up in the back of the car and pulled open his leather bag. He raised something overhead, and it seemed as if a white-hot light blazed from his hands.

Alex focused his binoculars. Commandant R. was holding a huge diamond shaped like a pyramid. The same diamond that Alex's uncle Jonathan had taken from Anubis's temple four years ago!

Alex groaned. His father had told Jonathan the gem would be trouble, but Jonathan hadn't cared. He had just wanted to impress the latest love of his life. Alex's dad insisted he sell it to the first buyer anyway. The last Alex had heard, the diamond was in a wealthy couples' home in Oxford.

"The Germans must have stolen it," Alex whispered.

As Commandant R. held the diamond, a black mist hurtled from the ground, rising hundreds of feet into the air. Within that mist a human face took shape, a face that howled in triumph. It was the Scorpion King. Alex's blood froze in his veins.

Now Alex knew that the Germans were offering Anubis his diamond back. But what did they want in return?

Commandant R. grinned at the monstrous Scorpion King and hurled the diamond into the sand. He shouted in German, and Ungricht began to translate his words into ancient Egyptian. Alex followed as best as he could. "The temple of Anubis has been defiled by our common enemies!" Commandant R. claimed. "I have come to return that which was stolen. I beg you to take this offering as a token of friendship between my master and your master."

The dark face gazed down at the diamond triumphantly, and its eyes closed, as if savoring the victory.

The ground began to tremble. A rumbling rose slowly, as faint as an earthquake striking a distant land. Then the valley shook in earnest, as if the world would split in half. Rocks tumbled from the cliffs above, bouncing past Alex. He covered his head with his hands.

Suddenly, morning sunlight played upon the diamond, blinding Alex with a brightness that seemed to come from a fire burning beneath it.

The flame grew, and Alex saw the truth: it wasn't a fire. It was gold, the golden pyramid-shaped temple, rising once again from the earth.

In seconds it heaved itself up from the ground. Rocks and dirt were shoved upward along with the pyramid. Dust and sand roiled in the air, and the golden temple glimmered like new. As the rocks and dirt rolled away, Ungricht threw the car into reverse. Tons of debris tumbled toward the spot where they had been parked.

But the cursed jungle from Alex's nightmares remained underground. *Things could be worse,* Alex thought, relieved.

And then they were.

From the sands around the temple there arose a tide of Anubis warriors. The vile creatures crawled up on skeletal hands, as if clawing their way out of their own graves. Their jackal heads yammered and howled in animal delight. The warriors stood before the temple, waving huge battleaxes overhead.

Alex stared in shock. Maybe the Scorpion King would keep the diamond and squash these wheedling little creeps.

The Germans looked terrified. Ungricht raced the engine on the car, inching it slowly backward. But the Anubis warriors did not advance.

An army of mummy guards shambled out from the temple's twin doors. Bits of bone and rotted tissue peeked out from their gray wrappings. Each guard carried an ancient Egyptian sword, a bronze weapon with a thick axlike tip, and held it high in salute. They formed two columns in front of the temple.

Then the Scorpion King strode from the bowels of his dark sanctuary, looking even more fierce than Alex remembered. His bare skull gleamed white in the sun, and his razor-sharp tail swung wildly. In his right claw, the Scorpion King bore the deadly Spear of Osiris.

"Ås tai-ten neb? Tuå hati shepå," the Scorpion King roared in ancient Egyptian. *Who is your master, that I might reward him?*

Commandant R. and Ungricht shouted in unison, "Adolf Hitler!"

"What reward does he desire?" the Scorpion King asked.

"He seeks power over death."

"Anubis claims the lives of all men," the Scorpion King replied. "Why should he not take the life of your master?"

Commandant R. answered proudly, "My lord Hitler is amassing the most powerful army this world has ever known. His men carry sticks that shoot thunder. He has steel elephants that spit fire. He has metal falcons that fly overhead dropping vast eggs of destruction. No enemy can withstand him—no enemy but time.

"If Anubis grants him favor, my lord Hitler promises to build a temple in his honor, a temple greater by far than the one that stands before us. The world shall once again worship the god of the underworld at its gates."

"Prove that you have such power," the Scorpion King demanded.

Three Anubis warriors slavered and growled like dogs as they began to lumber toward the car.

Commandant R. calmly drew his pistol from its holster, taking aim between the first monster's eyes. With a single shot, he felled the beast. He spun and aimed at a second warrior. Its head peeled back.

The third monster reached the car before Commandant R. could shoot it. Commandant R. didn't have time to aim. He merely drove it back with three bullets to the chest. Black blood gushed from its wounds. The warrior buried its ax in the car hood and roared in agony as it died.

As each warrior fell, the sands from which it was formed flowed back into the ground.

When he was done, Commandant R. waved the pistol and said, "I promise you, if Anubis grants the wish of my master, there will be such weapons for your warriors."

The Scorpion King smiled. "Great is the power of Hitler indeed, but it is not meant for man to live forever. We will give you an ankh that will let him reign for a thousand years on Earth, no more. In exchange, Hitler must make an offering to the god of the dead. He must sacrifice one of his beloved. The sacrifice must offer his soul to Anubis. Do you agree?"

Commandant R. nodded. "Hitler will be content if his rule over the Third Reich lasts for a thousand years. One soul is a small price to pay for world domination."

From the cliff, Alex heard Rachel give a soft cry of astonishment.

5

NOWHERE TO RUN

Alex wondered if the Germans had heard Rachel cry out. Things were getting worse and worse. Alex turned and began to sneak up through the rocks toward Rachel.

As he climbed, he fingered the signal mirror in his pocket. The concave glass was shaped like his mum's tea saucers. Ardeth Bay had given it to Alex before he set out on his journey.

"For thousands of years, my ancestors have used polished daggers to send messages across the Sahara. To wear the dagger of the Medjai is a great honor," Ardeth Bay had told him. "One day you will earn that right. For now, this mirror is your tool. If you need us, raise it toward the sun, and we will come."

It's time to call the Medjai, Alex thought. *But first, I have to find Rachel.*

Alex reached the top of the cliff behind the statue of Anubis. Rachel was gone!

Maybe she got scared and went back to the camel, Alex thought. But he doubted that Rachel would scare so easily.

From the narrow gully just above Alex came the sound of feet on rocks. Alex called softly, "Rachel?"

A huge mummy guard stepped out onto the trail from behind the rock, hissing through yellow teeth. It drew a curved saber and held it in a hand that had rotted down to bone. The monster rushed toward Alex.

Alex had no weapons. Desperately he called out, "*_Heru-ur-khenti-år-ti, aa_m qab ås-t heh!*" But the mummy kept charging.

Alex raised his hand to ward off any blow. His signal mirror flashed, bouncing sunlight off the mummy's bandages.

That's it! Alex raised his aim and sent brilliant light straight into the mummy's eyes. The curved mirror focused like a magnifying glass.

"Aaargh!" The mummy squinted and bellowed in rage. It rushed blindly, swinging its sword. Alex ducked. The blade whistled through the air and slashed through Alex's mirror, shattering it. Alex managed to hold onto a large shard of glass. The mummy prepared to swing again. Its toe caught on a rock, and it tripped. The mummy roared in outrage as it tumbled headlong over the cliff. Alex stood still for half a second, heart pounding.

"What has the mummy done to Rachel?" he whispered.

Alex looked up the narrow trail. Another mummy was lumbering toward him, its ancient bronze sword held with deadly intent. Alex aimed the mirror fragment and tried to flash its light in his enemy's eyes again.

The mummy growled, and though his words were jumbled and coarse, Alex found he could somehow understand the language of the underworld. "Surrender, foolish child," the mummy said, "or I will cut out your living guts and feed them handful by handful to the Eater of Souls!"

Behind this mummy, a third crept from the rocks. It dragged Rachel forward, holding a sharp sword at her throat.

"Run, Alex!" Rachel shouted. "Get away from here!"

But even if Alex had wanted to run, there was no place for him to go—except over the cliffs.

Alex could only raise his hands and surrender. The mummies grinned wickedly, revealing mouths full of rotten teeth.

6

CAPTURED!

"Surrender!" the mummy hissed. Alex raised his hands. He still held a jagged shard of the broken mirror.

I could use it as a knife, he thought.

"You know," Alex told the mummies, "you're making a big mistake. We're with them!" He licked his lips and nodded toward Commandant R.'s car, hoping the mummies might be suffering from brain rot.

"Really, camel breath?" a mummy guard hissed. "Then your master will be eager to see you." It limped up the trail, ragged bits of old bandages swaying with each step. "Nefai? Nefai, are you well?" it called over the cliff. But the ground was a hundred feet below, and Nefai had landed on the rocks.

The mummy turned back to Alex, hissing in rage.

"It wasn't my fault," Alex said. "He's the one who thought he could fly."

The mummy jabbed Alex's chest with the point of his sword. "Move, you jackal!"

Hands high, Rachel led the way through shadowed vales still cool from the night. Rocks rose like pillars on either side of them, and the air carried the metallic taste of dust and desert stone.

Each time Alex or Rachel slowed, the mummies shoved the swords into their backs.

"You know," Alex whispered to Rachel, "you could have screamed louder when they caught you. It's customary for girls to scream."

Rachel frowned. "Try screaming when someone has your mouth covered with a fat hand that smells like rotten goat dung," she gritted out. "Besides, *you* weren't supposed to come stumbling back and get caught."

She was right. Alex should have figured that this place would be well guarded.

"Got any bright ideas on how to escape?" Rachel asked.

"Nope."

"Next time your tongue wags," Alex's mummy guard growled, "I will cut it off. Then we will see how well it wiggles when it lies on a hot rock."

All too soon they reached the bottom of the cliff. The guards marched them to the body of Nefai, crumpled and small-looking on the rocks at the feet of the giant statue of Anubis. His dry bones had shattered, and Alex could see into his hollow belly cavity. A rat had built a nest there and then died sometime in ages past. Its bones lay there like a half-digested meal. The only internal organ left in the mummy was a heart so dried out and shrunken it was about the size of a walnut.

"Nefai was like a cousin to me," one mummy guard hissed. "He would want me to have his sword."

"A cousin?" the other mummy said. "He was more like a *brother* to me—closer even—a favored brother. He would want *me* to have his sword."

The first mummy nodded. "All right," he said, "but surely he would want me to have the canopic jar that holds his liver."

"Agreed," the second mummy replied. "But he would want me to have his gold ring."

"You know," Alex said, "those are pretty nice bandages he's wearing. Think he'd mind if I took them?"

Alex's guard growled, "Laugh while you can, mortal. Where you are going, only demons laugh."

The mummies took Nefai's valuables and then marched Alex and Rachel half a mile across the desert toward Ungricht's car. Two hundred yards south of that, the golden pyramid gleamed in the sun. Anubis warriors and mummies guarded its doors, though the horrid Scorpion King had already retreated inside.

Alex tried to imagine what Ungricht might do to them. As they got closer, the ground seemed to hiss. Black scorpions crawled out from under every stone and patch of sand, the sun gleaming on their backs. Millions of them scampered about as the party approached. They raised their pincers and stinging tails in a threatening pose.

"Well," Rachel told Alex, "you wanted to get a closer look at the scorpions. Is this close enough?"

"Yeah," Alex said, his throat dry.

But the creepiest thing about the scorpions wasn't their sheer number, it was how they moved, leaving a perfect little trail for the guards to follow—right to Ungricht's car.

Ungricht sat in the front seat with the top up to shade him from the sun, his skeletal face draped in shadows. Commandant R. paced beside the car with the grotesque little ghoul, Foot Rot, trailing slowly behind him.

"Well, well. What do have we here?" Commandant R. asked, smiling cruelly.

Ungricht climbed out of his seat like a zombie from a coffin. His skin was pale, almost white, as if he had died long ago. "So, you're the ones who attacked camp last night. Such brave children," he said, shaking his head. "Now you must pay."

The ghoul scurried toward them. "She's got some nice flesh on those bones," it hissed, "and he'll do nicely for dessert. You gut them. I'll cook."

Ungricht grinned and drew his fist back. Alex braced himself and prepared to duck.

Commandant R. grabbed his wrist. "Wait!" he ordered. "If you want to kill them, take them out in the desert and do it." He pulled his pistol from his holster.

No! Alex's heart raced. There had to be a way out.

Ungricht glanced at the weapon with distaste. "Not with that," he said. "Not when the sand is so warm and the scorpions are so hungry."

7

A SEA OF SCORPIONS

The mummy guards held their swords on Alex and Rachel as Ungricht got some rope from the car. "Put out a hand," he ordered Alex.

Alex still had the shard of broken mirror in his right hand, so he held out his left, palm open, and then made a fist, staring Ungricht in the eye as if he might slug him.

Ungricht grinned. "Ah, defiance—I like that quality in a man." He tied the rope tightly around his wrist. "Now the other."

Alex held out his right hand, palm down. Ungricht grinned as he bound it, then tied the ropes to Rachel's wrists.

"Now," Ungricht said joyfully, "where would you two like to die? Someplace where there is no shade, I think, so that you will get a good view of the sun. Someplace where there are a lot of scorpions."

He led the two prisoners two hundred yards west of camp, with the mummy guards and the horrid little ghoul shuffling along behind them. Scorpions blackened the ground like some nightmarish infestation. The scorpions backed away as the group approached.

Foot Rot hissed merrily, "I killed a man once by tying him in the sun. It took him two days to die. He would have lived longer, but the ants found him and started eating."

Ungricht eyed the scorpions with pleasure. "Here," he demanded, pointing to a small mound that rose above them. "Nail them down right here, Foot Rot."

Foot Rot didn't move. "You're not my master," he said, stubbornly.

Ungricht rolled his eyes. "Your master would like this spot. Trust me."

"Anything for the Scorpion King," Foot Rot replied, and began driving the stakes into the dirt.

"The sun will cook you all day," Ungricht told Alex. "And then, when you are too tired to move, the scorpions will begin to feed. They always sting their prey before they eat, you know. I watched a man die of a scorpion bite. He said that the poison burned like acid in the veins. No scorpion in the world is more dangerous than these."

Ungricht forced Rachel and Alex into place, then tied each wrist and ankle to a stake. "Unfortunately, I am afraid that when we leave, the scorpions will crawl under you. It can't be helped. You will make good shade for them, no? They will not eat you during the day, I think. They are creatures of the night—much like me!" He laughed. "So, you will sleep on a bed of scorpions. But I think they will not sting you, if you do not wiggle too much."

"Wait," Rachel begged. "You can't just kill us. You're the bad guy. You're supposed to tell us all about your evil plot for world domination before we die."

"World domination?" Ungricht laughed. "Hitler wants that. I'm only a humble servant who hopes to eat a few crumbs that drop from his table."

"You know, you're only getting a thousand years of rule for one soul," Alex said. "That's not a very good trade. Dinosaurs ruled the earth for *millions* of years, and they didn't have to pay a thing."

When Ungricht made no answer, Rachel asked, "So who is going to give his soul—Hitler?"

"Hitler come here?" Ungricht laughed. "He would not stoop so low. He is sending a trusted loyal SS officer, General H."

Rachel gasped, "He's a member of the Gestapo, Hitler's secret police. Is Hitler's policy of racial cleansing finally over?"

"Foolish child," Ungricht sighed. "We won't stop until we've driven all the Jews from Germany—along with the Slavs, Gypsies, blacks, and Armenians, of course. Then the German race will be pure. And if everything goes as planned, soon the whole world will be fit for our master race."

Rachel began to tremble.

"How are you going to get General H. to fall for this?" Alex asked. "I mean, you plan to use him as a human sacrifice. Won't he object if you stick a dagger in him?"

Ungricht laughed. "General H. knows the plan. Anubis demands a sacrifice, and General H. feels honored to give it. And the ordeal is not nearly as messy as a dagger in the back. General H. must simply breathe into a canopic jar. When he does, his soul will come out. The body will continue to live, though the soul is gone.

"Then Anubis will come to his temple, and he will give General H. a necklace with a medallion on it—an ankh. As long as General H. wears it, he will be protected from death and Hitler will rule for a thousand years. Without it"—Ungricht scowled—"the deal is off."

"What kind of life would it be without a soul?" Rachel asked.

"Pleasant enough," Ungricht said, as if he knew the answer personally. "There are little changes. You hardly notice them. The conscience leaves. One . . . forgets whatever little he knew about the difference between right and wrong. And there is a sense of loss. But all in all, it is not so bad."

Alex wondered to whom Ungricht had sold his soul, and for what reward.

As Ungricht tightened the last rope, Foot Rot grabbed an enormous scorpion from the ground. It wriggled as he held it, driving its stinger into the ghoul's rotted flesh. He laid it on Rachel's chest, and the scorpion merely sat for a moment, claws wide, as if unsure whether to attack.

"Do not try to escape," Foot Rot hissed. "The eyes of the Scorpion King are upon you."

"Goodbye, my friends," Ungricht whispered.

Alex and Rachel were left with only the sun above, the stone-hard dirt beneath, and the ground black with scorpions around them.

Once Ungricht and his fiends left the mound, the scorpions began to climb it, rising toward Alex and Rachel in a black tide.

8

CREATURES OF THE UNDERWORLD

At noon, flies crawled on Alex's lips. He twitched to clear the pests away. He and Rachel seemed so calm, considering the circumstances. Alex realized they were probably both in a state of disbelief. The huge scorpion on Rachel's chest jerked its tail upright and lurched forward, as if it would sting her.

"Keep still," Rachel warned him in a whisper. "I swear, if this bug kills me, I'll figure out some way to claw out of the grave and make you pay."

Each time Alex had moved, it was the same. It was as if the eyes of the Scorpion King really *were* watching them. Every twitch of his muscles brought the creature on guard.

Alex twisted just a little to sneak a peek toward camp. Scorpions crackled beneath him. As the day had begun to heat up, hundreds of them had crawled up the stake to sleep. Alex could feel them against his back, like small pebbles, shifting under him with each breath. One false move and they'd sting.

"We can't just wait to die," Alex told Rachel. "We've got to try something." The sun overhead was a demon, burning a hole through him. His face and arms ached from sunburn, and his tongue felt as if it were swelling in his throat. Heat was rising from the desert in waves.

Alex had never felt so tired. He'd not slept at all last night. For strength, he recalled the words of Ardeth Bay: "The Medjai must never tire of doing good. The powers we fight are too vast, too dangerous."

Alex still had his shard of glass in hand. He wanted to try to cut his bonds, but he hadn't dared. Not with the scorpion watching his every move and Ungricht lingering at the door of his tent, with guards on either side. Alex was sure that Ungricht hoped they would cry out and beg for mercy. Neither Alex nor Rachel gave him the pleasure.

Alex was waiting for nightfall, when the Germans couldn't see them. *But will we live that long?* Alex wondered, sweat dripping down his brow. They were in what the ancient Egyptians had called *Desh-ret,* the "red lands," the land of the dead. Few people could survive the heat here for even a day. Alex realized he had not had a drink since yesterday. He had not told Rachel last night, but he'd given her the last of his water.

"Look!" Rachel cried. A huge falcon hovered above them, its wings beating rapidly as it scanned the ground. Suddenly, the scorpion began to quiver. It turned its head toward the sky.

"Now's our chance!" Alex shouted.

Alex peeked toward the temple. The mummies and Anubis warriors were all gone!

Of course, he realized. *They're creatures of the underworld. They don't like the light.*

But where were Ungricht and Commandant R.? The only one in sight was Foot Rot, staring at Anubis's temple from the running board of Ungricht's car. The roof of the convertible was up, and the passenger door stood open. Alex shook his head, trying to fight off fatigue.

"That's it!" he whispered. "We didn't sleep at all last night. But the Germans didn't either. That's why they're so quiet! The only one on guard is that little ghoul, Foot Rot."

"And your point is?" Rachel asked, rolling her eyes.

"My point is that I have a piece of glass in my hand," Alex said. "If the falcon keeps your scorpion distracted, we just might have a chance of getting out of here."

"Ah," Rachel said. "I like the sound of it. I mean, the only guard in camp is a ghoul the size of a six-year-old. How tough can it be? After all, its muscles are rotted. Fighting it should be easy."

He glanced at Rachel. She talked like a trooper, but she looked terrible. Sunburn had blistered her face and cracked her parched lips. They had to get out of there. Fast. Alex began sawing through the ropes, running the glass back and forth quickly behind him.

"You know," Rachel whispered to the scorpion, "I'm very fond of crabs and shrimp. I've eaten dozens of your cousins. And right now I'm so hungry, I am thinking that when I get free, I might eat you, too!"

The huge scorpion suddenly went rigid and raised its tail. "Shhhh!" Alex whispered, freezing in place. The only sound came from the powerful falcon circling above. In ancient Egypt, the falcon was the symbol of the god Horus, who triumphed over evil. Ardeth Bay had taught Alex a spell that was supposed to summon the falcon's aid.

Alex closed his eyes and whispered, *"Heru-nefer . . ." Horus, I beg refuge.*

Immediately, the falcon dove in a streak of feathers that fell like lightning from the sky. It grabbed the huge scorpion, then shot off again into the air, crunching the wriggling creature in its claws.

Alex heard a roar like distant thunder. It was barely audible and came from inside the golden pyramid. The voice of the Scorpion King shouted, "My eyes! My eyes!"

Underneath them, swarms of scorpions began to scramble toward the temple.

"The Scorpion King is awake!" Rachel shouted.

"All right, Foot Rot," Alex said. "Here we come."

9

FIGHTING THE GHOUL

Alex managed to slash the cords that bound his right wrist, quickly free the left, and cut the cords on his feet.

"Come on, Rachel, it's time to go." Alex rolled over and slashed her bonds, giddy with fatigue.

"Really?" she said. "Just when the party was starting to heat up?"

Alex climbed to his feet and raced toward Foot Rot, keeping to the other side of the car to shield them from the ghoul's view. The ghoul was a head shorter than Alex, but it had a powerful frame. On closer inspection, it was easy to see that Foot Rot suffered from more than just foot decay. Its stringy hair had fallen out by the handful. Its left ear had rotted off. Flies had laid eggs on its naked skull, and maggots crawled there.

"Maybe I should have nicknamed you Brain Rot," Alex whispered, grinning. He glanced into the car. The keys were in the ignition. Alex's dad had taught him to drive on his last birthday—Egypt had few cars and even fewer driving laws.

Rachel raced up behind Alex.

From the golden pyramid, a second shout followed, even louder. "My eyes! My eyes!" Alex realized with rising dread that the Scorpion King was leaving his underground cave. He would bring Anubis warriors and mummies with him by the thousands!

The ghoul heard the cries now and leapt off the running board of the car. It whirled around to look at Alex, flies rising from it in a cloud.

"Now we're in trouble," Alex muttered, and started to back away.

"No one defies the Scorpion King," the ghoul roared in outrage, and raised its hand. It had a pistol!

Foot Rot shouted at the gun in ancient Egyptian, "Kill them!"

Alex leapt to the right just as bullets flew from the pistol barrel and whipped past his head. The recoil from the gun knocked Foot Rot back onto the ground.

"Well," Alex said, "I guess we can't sneak around anymore."

Alex and Rachel jumped aside, using the car to protect themselves.

From the tent, Commandant R. shouted, "*Angriff! Angriff!*"

Foot Rot growled at Rachel, "Hold still, you slithering mongoose!" The little zombie started to climb into the cab of the car to get at her.

Alex did the only thing he could think of. He rolled over the hood and slammed the car door closed on the rotten monster.

The weight of the door nearly chopped Foot Rot in two. Rachel shouted, "I'll get the gun!" She reached in from the window and tried to pull it from the monster's hands. But the zombie wasn't dead.

"So, you want to play rough!" it screamed. "How is this for rough?" The ghoul shot twice at Rachel, drilling holes through the metal door.

"Peace," Alex shouted in ancient Egyptian. "I'm a friend?" he added, trying to calm the ghoul.

The ghoul tore at the door handle, screaming in pain. It got the door open again and collapsed on the ground, its nearly severed legs still kicking.

"Look what you did, you nasty little dung beetle!" the zombie swore. "Do friends chop friends in half where you come from? I'm going to suck your eyes out!"

As the creature crawled toward Alex on its hands, Alex jumped over it and into the driver's seat. Rachel slid into the back. The ghoul screamed in outrage and wrenched its neck as it turned to look for them.

Just then, Alex glanced in the rearview mirror. Commandant R. and Ungricht were racing from the tent! Commandant R. held a rifle.

The ghoul spotted the movement. "Now I've got you, goat breath!" he shouted, firing blindly.

It was a good thing for Alex that the ghoul didn't know how to aim. The bullet just missed Commandant R.

"Swine!" Commandant R. shouted, and returned fire.

The next thing Alex knew, the ghoul was blasting away at the tent, its eyes shut tight.

Amid the confusion, Alex shifted the car into neutral, putting one foot on the clutch and the other on the gas. He turned the key.

Ungricht began shouting at Foot Rot in ancient Egyptian, "Not us! Not us! Get the boy in the car!"

"No," Alex yelled at the ghoul. "Get the guys in the tent!"

Alex shifted the car into first gear and floored it. A cloud of red dust spat out from the rear tires as the car lunged forward.

A bullet smashed through the rear window. Alex ducked. "Yikes! That was close!" Bullets slammed into the trunk of the car, sounding like rocks bashing tin cans.

"Go, Alex!" Rachel shouted. She lurched across the back seat and began trying to roll up the back window as the car lumbered over the ground.

Alex heard an ominous noise and glanced at the side-view mirror. Foot Rot had grabbed the door handle and was clinging to it. *Hiss!* The creature bared its pointed teeth and waved its pistol in Rachel's face.

"What's wrong with this stupid thing?" Foot Rot roared in frustration. It was pulling the pistol trigger over and over, but the gun had run out of bullets.

Alex only hoped that the ghoul didn't crawl through the window and get them. Another bullet whipped past his head and blew apart the rearview mirror. Someone shot one of the tires, and the car veered left. Foot Rot clung to the swerving car and howled in outrage.

"Sorry!" Alex shouted at the ghoul.

The roaring inside the temple continued, and the Scorpion King suddenly appeared at the door. He squinted in pain, as if his eyes had just been ripped out. The Spear of Osiris gleamed in his claws, and the sun shone on the bleached skull. The stinger above his back swayed and lashed, as if seeking a victim.

"Rise, my warriors!" the Scorpion King roared. "Stir your rotten bones. Bring forth your weapons and avenge your lord! The boy is mine!"

His voice echoed from the hills like thunder. Across the desert, the sand began to rise again, taking the shape of jackal-headed warriors. They clawed their way from the ground, howling and roaring like a rising storm. Their misshapen bodies and grisly faces were more terrifying than before.

"You know, I really don't think we're welcome here!" Rachel said. "I'm ready to leave when you are."

Alex floored the gas pedal, but the car still didn't move fast enough to suit him.

Foot Rot suddenly pulled himself through the half-open window and plopped into Alex's lap. His entire lower body had fallen off. Dried stringy guts spilled from him. "I'm going to eat your ears!" the ghoul shouted at Alex and tried to take a bite.

"Get off me, you stinking bag of bones!" Alex yelped. "I've had enough of you!"

He grabbed the monster by its neck and shoved it toward the window. Rachel punched the little scrap of rotting hide, knocking it clean out of the car. It bounced on a pile of rocks.

"I'll get you if it's the last thing I do!" the ghoul roared in outrage.

Alex veered from the temple and sped away as fast as he could. He couldn't have driven fast enough, not with two flat tires, the Germans taking shots every time he put his head above the dashboard, and the Scorpion King galloping behind the car on six ugly legs, with an army of Anubis warriors in tow.

As the car topped a small hill, Rachel told Alex, "Let's hop on your camel and ride! I don't want to slow down till we reach Cairo!"

"No," Alex said. "We can't leave yet. General H. is coming to the temple tonight to make a sacrifice. If he gets the ankh, Hitler will take over the world and reign for a thousand years. We must stop him!"

10

THE WAR BEGINS

"You mean that you want to go back?" Rachel demanded. "After what they did to us?"

"Yes," Alex said. "I *have* to fight them—now more than ever!" He was sworn to fight against those who would waken the evil powers that lived in the tombs. "But you're free to leave if you want. You can have my camel."

He glanced behind the car as it rattled across the desert. He could see no sign of the Scorpion King in his mirror. The bullets had quit flying once he topped the last little hill. But with the front tires blown, he couldn't go fast, and the car shook outrageously each time it hit a rock.

Rachel swallowed hard, fighting back her fear. "All right," she finally said, shaking. "I'll fight them with you."

"Are you sure?" Alex asked in surprise.

"I did not tell you everything," Rachel said, biting her lip. "When the Germans burned our house, my mother was still inside. She did not make it out."

Alex's face went white. "I'm so sorry."

"General H. and his secret police did that to my mother," Rachel said. "I have declared war on him!"

"No," Alex corrected. "*We* have declared war on him!"

Alex pulled the car into the shade of a rock by his camel. For a moment he felt safe. The Scorpion King and the Germans were nearly three miles behind.

"They'll follow us, you know," Alex said. "The Anubis warriors will hunt us."

"I know. We'll just have to come up with a plan."

"If we make it look like we've run away, we can circle back to camp under cover of darkness."

"What then?" Rachel asked.

"We have to break into the temple," Alex said. "And make sure that General H. doesn't make a bargain with Anubis."

There would be warriors and mummies in the temple. Worse, Anubis himself would come.

"Do we have any water?" Rachel asked.

"No," Alex said. "The Germans got my canteen. But there are some pomegranates in my saddlebag."

Rachel climbed out of the car and went to the saddlebags.

Alex took stock of the situation. Stinkwad sat in the shade nearby, twitching his ears. In his bags, Alex had a little Medjai survival kit—a compass, a map, some dried dates, nuts. Nothing that he could use as a weapon.

As Rachel got a pomegranate, she said, "The commandant had a radio in the trunk. We should not let him get it back. Otherwise, he will use it to guide the general's plane down for a landing."

"Right," Alex agreed. He wondered what else the Germans might have left behind. Alex got out of the car and peered into the trunk. A keg of gasoline and some blankets. But there was something underneath.

"Eureka!" he shouted. "We've hit the mother lode!"

"Water?" Rachel asked eagerly.

"Even better." Beneath the blankets were a canteen, cans of sauerkraut, a flare gun, a medical kit, a knife, a wrench, a spare tire, and a tire jack.

Alex dragged the food out and opened all eight cans of sauerkraut. Quickly they gulped down a cold meal.

What would the Medjai do? he thought, staring at the supplies. "Every object has a purpose," Alex whispered, remembering his lessons.

Then he got the spare tire and some wire cutters from the tool kit and began cutting the tire into small squares. He emptied the cans and put a square of tire in each one. "Fill each can half full of gas. Use tape from the medical kit to put the lids back on, but leave a hole for a fuse."

"What are we making?" Rachel asked.

"Smoke bombs. The temple is a closed building and the rubber tires are filthy. When they burn—" Alex smiled—"they'll fill the air with dirt."

"Right," Rachel nodded. "General H. won't be making any bargains if he can't breathe."

"Besides, mummies are afraid of fire. They burn like that," Alex said, snapping his fingers. "When they died, their bodies were covered with natron, a kind of salt that dried them out, and then they were wrapped in bandages. So all the water dried out of them thousands of years ago."

"Remind me again how you know all this," Rachel sighed.

"From my mum. She knows everything about ancient Egypt. She told me that back in England in the olden days—like fifty years ago—people used to throw tea parties at Christmas and unwrap mummies for fun, just to see if they could find any gold rings or pins on them. When they were done, they would throw the mummies into the yule fire and let them burn. Sometimes, because coal was so expensive, they would sell mummies to the railroad, to burn for train fuel."

Rachel shook her head. "Has anyone ever told you you're a little odd?"

"I'll take that as a compliment." Alex grinned and continued cutting up the tire, slicing the inner tube into long bands. He pulled one rubber band experimentally.

"What now?" she asked. "You're not making a slingshot, are you?"

"It's the best thing we've got," Alex answered. "Unless you're hiding a weapon in your pocket."

"*No,* but I can make one," Rachel said without

hesitation. She grabbed the wrench from the tool kit and rolled under the car. Within seconds, she had pulled out a metal rod shaped like a Y. It was about a foot long. "This should work as a post," she said, handing it to Alex. "Now all we need is ammunition."

Alex gaped. "Um, thanks." He removed the burned wheels from the car and took out the heavy ball bearings. As he tied the inner tubes to the metal Y, Rachel nodded in approval. Alex's slingshot was huge. The ball bearings were solid steel, an inch around.

Alex pulled the tailpipe off the car and eyed it critically.

"What are you going to do with *that*?" Rachel asked.

"I was thinking that maybe I could turn it into a flamethrower."

"You know," Rachel said, "when you grow up, I think you could have a great career as a mad scientist."

In the distance, Alex heard the yapping and yowling of jackals. He glanced back toward the

Temple of Anubis. Commandant R. and Ungricht were marching across the desert, leading more than a dozen mummies and Anubis warriors.

"Quick," Alex said as he loaded the flare gun and shoved it into his belt. "Let's hide these weapons before Commandant R. and the others get here!"

Rachel grabbed the smoke bombs and slingshot and carried them to the top of the rock pile. Alex brought the medical kit and blankets, then ran back to the car.

Rachel covered the supplies with the blanket, then piled on rocks and dirt to hide them better. "Hurry!" she warned Alex.

"Just a minute," he shot back.

"We don't have a minute."

Rachel was right. The Anubis warriors were getting close. Alex inserted one end of a long gauze bandage from the medical kit into the gas tank. Then, as if it were the wick of an oil lamp, he lit the other end of the cloth.

"Okay," he said. "Let's get out of here—fast! Once the flame hits the fumes coming out of the gas tank, this car is going to explode!"

"Thanks for the warning," Rachel said.

They ran to Stinkwad and climbed on. Alex prodded the camel to his feet and headed west down a long slope, deeper into the desert. Minutes later, they climbed over the top of a sand dune, and Alex stopped the camel. They sat watching the rock pile a quarter of a mile back.

Their pursuers were close. Anubis warriors yapped like a pack of hunting dogs. With their long legs, they'd outpaced Ungricht and Commandant R. They howled in delight and raced to the car just as it exploded. The fireball hurled the warriors five feet in the air. Afterward, the car belched black smoke.

"You have changed nothing!" Commandant R. shouted at them. "You have won nothing. General H. will come."

Ungricht strode forward. "Anubis has many who serve him. We will hunt you down!"

Alex turned the camel and raced over the dunes, fleeing into the desert.

11

IN RAMLAT EL KEBIR

Alex and Rachel rode across the Sahara, heading west from the golden pyramid of Anubis into Ramlat el Kebir, the Great Sea of Sand. Alex hoped the sand would slow the warriors down.

Golden dunes surged up like hills, and with each step, the camel's wide hooves slipped. The desert was endless. Alex remembered hearing the Medjai describe Ramlat el Kebir: There is sand, and sand piled upon sand, and more sand–stretching so far that even Allah's all-seeing eyes must squint to see across it.

It was a threatening place. The nearest water was a two-day ride by camel, and anyone who tried to walk across that waste would not last a day.

The spit in Alex's mouth ran dry.

Rachel wrapped a blanket over her head to keep

out the sun and leaned against Alex's back, her arms wrapped around his waist. Alex had never had a girl wrap her arms around him, at least no one other than his mother.

"Have you figured out how to get into the temple?" Rachel asked.

"Let's wait and see how many guards there are," Alex said. "The Anubis warriors and mummies are creatures of the night. They'll come out by the thousands at sunset under the Scorpion King's command."

"Hmmm . . . ," Rachel mumbled tiredly. She soon fell silent and began to breathe deeply.

Alex felt exhausted. He had barely slept in the past forty hours, but he didn't dare close his eyes. *The Medjai are tireless,* he told himself. *And I want to be a Medjai.* But this was more than Alex had bargained for when he began his Mushwâr Wa, his lone walk. He wanted Ardeth Bay.

Yapping cut across the silence. Alex glanced over his back and saw a dark line on the horizon.

"Oh no!" he muttered. Five miles back, at least a hundred Anubis warriors were marching toward him with battleaxes on their shoulders. He could see no sign of the Germans or Foot Rot.

Alex prodded the camel to hurry and raced deeper into the endless sea of dunes, until he could no longer see the fierce warriors.

Near sundown, he rode to the top of an enormous dune and looked out over the rolling hills of sand. A warm wind whipped dust into the air. There were few things more menacing than a storm in the desert, and one was brewing in the distance. He could smell it. It would not be a wet storm with clouds and lightning. It would be a windstorm, with sheets of sand that could scour the flesh off your bones.

Alex licked his parched lips and found the piece of broken signal mirror in his pocket. He held it high and flashed a message toward the setting sun, calling for help from any Medjai who might see it. "Please, Ardeth Bay," he whispered, "if you can see this, answer me. . . ."

Alex waited anxiously for a reply. But there were no answering flashes from the Medjai's silver knives.

"It doesn't mean that they are not there," he told himself. "The sun is setting, and the wind is fierce. Even if someone saw my call for help, they might not be able to send a message back."

As the sun dipped behind the dunes, he turned the camel back toward the Temple of Anubis and dropped into a valley filled with shadows.

12

DEAD EYES NEVER BLINK

Alex finally brought the weary camel to a stop a few hours later.

Rachel stretched groggily, wiping sand from her face. "Where are we?"

"Back at Anubis's temple. Our supplies should be right above these dunes," Alex said, handing Rachel the binoculars. "Here, I'll show you."

They climbed off the camel and walked to the edge of the sand. Rachel raised the binoculars toward their rock pile and let out a startled cry.

"What's wrong?"

"There's a bunch of five-thousand-year-old mummies sitting on top of our blankets."

"How many?" Alex whispered.

"At least three." Rachel passed the binoculars back to Alex. "See for yourself."

A mummy crouched with a sword in its hand,

gazing straight at them. The bandages had fallen off its face long ago; only bits of ragged flesh still clung to its yellowed skull. At the base of the rock pile, Alex could see two other mummies—one to the right and one to the left. The shadows were too deep to tell if more hid there.

He ducked his head down. "We need those supplies. We'll just have to fight them."

"But they have swords," Rachel warned.

"The good thing about mummies," Alex whispered, "is that most of them are more than half rotted. Their muscles are rotted, so they aren't very strong. Their brains are rotted, so they aren't very smart. As long as we don't panic, we should be able to beat them. Unless . . . ," Alex fell silent.

"Unless what?"

"Some mummies know magic."

"Magic? Like they pull rabbits out of their hats?"

"I wish it were only that," Alex said. "My dad told me about a man who opened a mummy's coffin, and the mummy cast a spell on him. All at once, the man was full of maggots."

"You mean his stomach was full, like he had eaten maggots?"

"No," Alex warned, "I mean his eyes, his liver, and his brains were full. He started coughing them up and screaming. He only got about fifty feet before he died."

"Disgusting!" Rachel shuddered.

"The point is," Alex said, "it's hard to understand what mummies say, but if you ever hear one start to utter a curse, you hit him quick and hit him hard."

Alex crawled across the sand dune to his saddlebags and pulled out a small knife. "Take this," he said. "When we reach the mummies, strike for the throat. The best way to kill a mummy is to take off its head."

"What about you?" she asked. "You don't have a weapon."

Alex raised his camel prod. It was a stout stick, about four feet long with a sharp metal tip. "I'll club them with this."

They climbed back on the camel, and Alex patted the weary beast. "Okay, Stinkwad," he whispered. "Do your stuff." He nudged the camel's sides with his heels and the stinking animal raced up the dune.

Suddenly, the horrid mummy guard roared a warning and leapt to its feet, pointing its sword at them. Two other mummies swarmed out of the shadows.

Stinkwad wheezed from strain as his hooves pounded the hard dirt. Rachel held Alex around the waist with one hand and clutched the dagger in the other. The mummies raised their swords and began to hiss.

"They're trying to scare us off!" Alex shouted.

"They're doing a good job!" Rachel said.

Their leader seemed to be the big mummy on top of the rocks. He pointed at Alex with his sword and shouted to his troops, *"Maim! Maim!"*

"What's he saying?" Rachel asked.

"Destroy!" Alex answered, shaking his head. "Not if we destroy them first!"

Alex charged. One mummy raced to the far side of the rock pile. The other mummy screamed in terror and hurled its sword. Alex ducked. The sword tumbled end over end past Rachel's ear.

Alex raced toward the mummy that had thrown the sword. He held his camel prod like a polo stick and swung at the mummy's head. The head exploded with a dry, papery sound, as if he had bashed a wasp's nest.

"I want to try that!" Rachel shouted. Stinkwad wheeled and galloped over the headless mummy. The mummy crunched under a hoof.

Alex glanced back and saw the mummy lying there with a camel's footprint in its back.

From the rock pile, Alex heard the big mummy leader begin to chant: *"Ånp neb-Tatchesertt, uha—"*

He was a sorcerer! "Quick Rachel," Alex cried. "Now's your chance!"

Rachel hurled her dagger with all her might. The blade flashed in the starlight. It struck the mummy leader in the chest, knocking him from his rocky perch. "Aaargh!" he cried, falling over.

"Good throw!" Alex said.

"Finish him!" Rachel shouted. Stinkwad spun toward the last two mummies on the far side of the rock pile.

The mummy leader stood there, looking dazed. It had regained its feet and pulled the knife from its chest. The mummy raised the knife blade so that it flashed in the starlight. *"Ånp neb-Tatchesertt—"*

"Shut up!" Alex said as he threw down his camel prod and leapt from the saddle. He landed on top of the mummy leader. Alex's weight smashed the pest, knocking the air from its lungs.

"Buha!" the mummy leader swore. *"Anaa!"*

"What?" Alex shouted back. "At least I don't have maggots in my nose!" Alex gritted his teeth and began wrestling with the mummy.

Rachel reined the camel to a halt just as Alex called, "Rachel, help! His breath is killing me!"

The mummy leader was on top of Alex, straining to bite Alex's nose off even as it worked the knife toward his heart. Alex gripped the leader's neck with one hand and fought for control of the knife with the other.

"Seriously, help!" Alex begged, fighting to get his nose away from the mummy's yellow teeth. "You've never smelled a dog with worse breath than this."

"Here I come, Alex!" Rachel jumped to the ground and grabbed Alex's camel prod. She swung it at the back of the leader's head like a baseball bat. "Take that, you nasty oaf!" She struck so hard that a couple of scarab beetles flew out of the mummy's mouth.

The mummy leader turned to look up at Rachel and hissed, *"Ni hebai!"*

"What did he say?" Rachel asked.

"He said," Alex answered in a strangled voice, "you hit like a girl."

"Oh yeah?" Rachel said. "Well, tell me if this hurts!" She slammed the camel prod down on the leader's head with all her might. The blow landed with a crusty sound, as if she'd just bashed in a dry loaf of bread, and snapped the mummy's head in half.

The leader went still. A dozen scarab beetles raced out of the crack in its head and scampered away from Alex.

The last mummy guard lunged out from behind the rocks, growling.

Rachel whirled around to face him. The mummy raised its sword, ready to lop off her head. Rachel's eyes opened wide in fright.

Suddenly, Alex's camel let out a grunt and rushed the last mummy. It bit the monster's wrist, snapping it in two.

"Way to go, Stinkwad!" Alex shouted.

The mummy shrieked in terror. Stinkwad raced forward and stomped it into the ground.

Alex groaned and threw the mummy leader off his chest. He climbed to his feet, winded.

"Are you all right?" Alex asked.

"Yes," Rachel gasped, catching her breath. "I just . . . give me a minute, and I'll be ready to bash a few more of them."

Alex grinned. "Good work. There are three creeps that won't be crawling out of their crypts anymore."

"Your—your camel—Stinkwad," Rachel stammered, "helped kill those mummies!"

"I trained him well," Alex said. "After all, he's going to be a Medjai's camel." He stood proudly with his black turban in the starlight, the rough wind making his robes billow out. He drew his knife from the mummy sorcerer's dead hands and slipped it into his belt.

"So he runs fast and kills mummies?" Rachel said, giving him a long look. "I think your camel is smelling sweeter by the minute."

"Give him enough time," Alex said, "and you'll think his sweat smells as sweet as the desert."

He looked to the temple below them. Blowing sand and the darkness were beginning to block the view. "They'll have guards," he said quietly. "We'd better make sure they don't get suspicious."

He grabbed the mummy leader and dragged it to the top of the rock, setting it up so that it faced the desert. "Perfect," he said as he finished.

He had other plans for the remaining mummy guards.

13
THE RISING STORM

By midnight, sheets of sand hung like ragged curtains across the sky, and the wind moaned in their ears. There was still no sign of the Medjai.

Rachel wrapped her robe more tightly around her and turned to Alex. "The storm is getting bad, no?" she asked.

"Not too bad yet," Alex said. "When clouds of sand start blowing above like thunderheads, then we're in trouble. The sand builds static electricity until lightning flashes. A storm like that is worse than any thunderstorm you've ever seen."

Alex spied on the temple through binoculars, looking for a way in. Two rows of bonfires burned in front, lighting a path to the temple's door. The gold pyramid reflected the fires' flickering light. A thousand Anubis warriors with huge battleaxes stood at the base of the temple, while mummies wandered between the fires, playing music on horns and drums.

It looked like the mummies were going to throw a party.

"You know," Alex told Rachel, "these mummies really seem excited to have a human sacrifice."

"Of course they're excited," Rachel said with a grin. "After all, they don't get out much! How would you like to be stuck in a tomb for five thousand years?"

"Boring," Alex answered. "Nothing to do all day but count the cockroaches . . ." He searched the night sky. He couldn't see any lights from a plane. He couldn't hear any droning engine. The sky held only a few stars and drifting sand.

Alex turned the binoculars toward the Germans' tent. Ungricht stood next to a lantern. He had shaved all the hair from his head and was dressed in black robes with a red sash so that he looked like a priest of Anubis. Foot Rot, now legless, hunkered on the ground washing his master's feet—a cleansing ritual that would let Ungricht officiate in the temple.

"I don't see Commandant R.," Alex told Rachel.

"I'll bet he is hunting for us," Rachel whispered.

Alex didn't like the sound of that, but he knew she was probably right. Commandant R. would be fuming. But where would he hunt?

Alex searched around the temple grounds, but all he could see were the bases of the creepy statues of Anubis.

"Does the pyramid have a back door?" Rachel asked.

"Pyramids don't have back doors," Alex replied. "The main part is underground. Anubis is a god of the underworld."

"But you do have a plan for getting in," Rachel said. "Right?"

He did, but Rachel wasn't going to like it. "Getting in should be easy," Alex promised. "It's getting out alive that I'm worried about."

14

DEADER THAN YOUR AVERAGE MUMMY

"So this is your plan?" Rachel demanded. She held the flashlight and watched in horror as Alex finished cutting the bandages from the head of one of the mummies they had killed. He pulled the wrap off. After so many years of rotting in a tomb, most of the mummy's skin came off with a tearing sound.

"It's a good plan," Alex said. "All we have to do is scrape off the nose and ears, and the bandage will fit over our faces like a mask." He turned the bandages inside out and started scraping away bits of flesh that clung to the inside. "See?"

The unwrapped mummy stared accusingly at them. Rachel fought back a shudder. "Don't worry," Alex told her. "This guy is deader than your average mummy."

Alex held the rotting bandages up to her face.

"I'm not going to put that on!" Rachel said. "It smells worse than Stinkwad."

"You'll get used to it," Alex said, wrapping the bandages around her face.

"There's only so much torture a nose can take," Rachel sighed, squirming.

"Hold still," Alex said, as he used a little tape from the medical kit to hold the mask in place. "I've only got a few more pieces to go."

"Alex," Rachel said, scratching at the bandages. "I think there's a bug in my mask."

Alex placed some bandages on her arms. "You lay on a bed of scorpions this morning," he said. "A few more bugs won't hurt."

"What if it is a scorpion?" she asked.

"Can't be," Alex said. "He would have stung you already."

"What else could it be then?" Rachel asked in rising panic. "I heard a story once about a girl who got an earwig in her ear. The earwig couldn't back out, and so it had to chew its way through to the other side."

"You've probably just got a termite in there with

you," Alex said. "Happens every time a mummy gets a little water on it."

"*That's* supposed to make me feel better?" Rachel groaned.

Alex tried to pull a bandage over Rachel's hand as if it were a glove, but there was still something inside. He went back to work scraping the fingers out of the mummy's bandage. Once he finished, he put it on her, and then Rachel helped Alex tape on his own mummy costume.

"How well can you see and hear in there?" Alex asked when they finished.

"I can see fine," Rachel said. "But you'll have to talk loud."

Alex agreed. The sound was definitely muffled. The wind howled mournfully, spattering sand on Alex's mask. Beneath that howl, Alex heard a rumbling. Bright lights sped among the stars.

"General H.'s plane!" Alex cried. "Hurry!"

15

DEAD MAN'S PARTY

"Okay," Alex whispered to Rachel as they approached the temple. "Try to act natural."

Alex bent his fingers into claws and opened his mouth wide, as if his jaw had just come unhinged. He started groaning and moaning as he crept forward.

"*That's* natural?" Rachel asked.

"It's natural for a mummy," Alex said. "Four years ago, the museum my mum worked at was swarming with them."

"Okay, okay," Rachel sighed. "I'll take your word for it."

The fields around the temple were full of scorpions. With every step, Alex heard them crunch under his bandaged feet.

"All right," Alex said, "we're coming to the crowd." He glanced back to make sure that Rachel was keeping up. In the dim firelight, Rachel was trying to walk like a mummy. It looked like she was doing some weird dance. "If we get separated, I'll meet you in the temple."

General H.'s plane was circling, getting lower and lower, but the mummies hadn't gotten the landing field cleared yet.

"*Tesh! Tesh!*—Hurry!" Ungricht shouted at the mummies, his robes flying out like raven's wings in the wind. With his pale head shaved bald, he looked more like a skeleton than ever.

The mummies finished picking up the rocks, and the plane came in for a landing. Its engines roared, and its bright headlights washed over the upraised heads of the mummies, giving everything a supernatural glow. The drums echoed louder. Shrill flutes sliced the night air like whistling swords. Horns blew in a crescendo. The mummies—thousands of them—began chanting.

Jostling with mummies at every step, Alex kept thinking about Rachel's strange walk.

"You know, Rachel," he whispered over his shoulder, "the trick to walking like a mummy is letting the joints in your knees and ankles sort of roll around. Just imagine that all the muscles in there have either dried up or fallen off."

Suddenly, a half-rotted mummy grabbed Alex by the throat and growled. Alex lurched away from the monster and tripped over another mummy.

"I–I was j-j-ust saying," Alex stammered, regaining his balance, "you have to try and blend in more. Like me–" Alex turned around to see if Rachel was listening. The only thing behind him was Commandant R.'s broad back–pushing Rachel away from him!

16
INTO THE TEMPLE

"I've caught the girl!" Commandant R. shouted, holding a pistol to Rachel's throat.

Foot Rot crawled behind Rachel, his dry guts still trailing from his severed torso.

"So, you were right," Ungricht said, striding through the crowds toward Rachel. "The foolish girl has returned." He stabbed his staff into the ground and stared down at Rachel. "Shall I feed her to the scorpions?"

Alex peered out from behind a temple pillar, his heart hammering in his chest. *Now what?* he wondered.

"You can have your fun later," Commandant R. said. "For now, we have other duties."

The plane had come to a stop fifty feet in front of Alex. Its light shone on the temple and blowing sand. Alex patted his mummy bandages gratefully. *At least I'm disguised,* he thought.

Just then, the door to the plane swung open and General H. appeared. He wore an SS uniform on his tall frame, and his cold eyes glimmered in the fire-light.

Mummies groaned and called out, *"Heru, Heru!"* General H. smiled and raised his hands, expecting applause.

Ungricht marched up to the plane and spoke briefly to General H. Alex couldn't hear their words over the chanting of the mummies. The two men turned and strode toward the pyramid. Alex stood tall and prayed they wouldn't notice his sagging costume.

The door to the pyramid gaped like a vast mouth. Anubis warriors with broad chests and gleaming axes barred the way. As General H. approached, the monsters bowed and stepped aside.

Commandant R. shoved his pistol into Rachel's back and ordered, "Come. We must follow them."

Alex wanted to grab Rachel as she passed, but there was no way. The path ahead sloped down through a forest of pillars, where flickering torches lit the passage.

Thunder boomed in the distance. Billowing clouds of sand were blotting out the stars. *Even if Ardeth Bay saw my signal, how will he make it here in time?* Alex sighed. *It's up to me.*

With the thousand other mummies who began filing into the temple for shelter, Alex shambled past the jackal-headed warriors that stood guard.

17
THE SHAPE OF A DARK SOUL

Alex stumbled into the temple, past a pair of golden statues of Anubis that rose on either side, past pillars and walls covered with hieroglyphs. Fog hovered in the air, so Alex could barely see Commandant R. and Ungricht leading the way.

Hundreds of mummies and Anubis warriors crowded close behind him. In time, the path ran out and became a crude trail through a cavern. The stale air held a thick, coppery scent, like blood. Stalactites hung like icicles from the roof, replacing the glorious pillars. Hot springs full of sulfur water bubbled beside the trail. A perfect temple for the god of the underworld.

At last, they reached a silent cavern where a black stone lay like a curved moon, its horns pointing upward. It was an altar where sacrifices would be made. The room was as quiet as any tomb. This was the Holy of Holies.

Alex ducked behind a crowd of mummies and stared at the altar. A pale blue light hung above it, shining down on a gorgeous vase. Dark bits of ebony were inlaid on its surface in complex patterns. It was a canopic jar, like the ones used to store the guts of mummies.

The horrible Scorpion King stood before the altar, his gleaming tail arched over his back. In the dim light, his body looked almost as if it were encased in armor. *"Nana,"* he said. *Welcome.* He motioned with the Spear of Osiris for General H. to come forward.

Mummies filed into the back of the chamber, forming a circle around the altar, filling the stale air with the smell of their dry rot.

Alex watched Rachel search desperately among the faces for any sign of him. *Over here,* he thought, wishing he could speak.

Ungricht addressed General H. "Now, you must kneel. Chant with me: *'Ånp neb-Tatchesertt, bak n m netr netri!'* You must repeat it thirteen times."

"Must I?" General H. asked. "What does it mean?"

" 'Oh, Dark Lord of the Grave, fill us with your power divine.' "

General H. knelt and began to chant. *"Ånp neb-Tatchesertt, bak n m netr netri. Ånp neb-Tatchesertt, bak n m netr netri. Ånp neb-Tatchesertt, bak n m netr netri."*

All around the room, mummies began to raise the chant, their words hanging like cobwebs in the still air.

Alex watched impatiently. He had to stop this devilish bargain, or Hitler would keep mankind enslaved for a thousand years. But how could he without Ardeth Bay? Alex breathed deeply and tried to swallow his fear. He had to think like a Medjai.

Alex's weapons were hidden in an ancient cloth sack he'd found on one of the dead mummies. He reached into the sack and clutched his flare gun, waiting for the right moment to strike.

A dark mist began to pour from the altar, filling the room with a fog blacker than smoke. The darkness deepened, and Alex thought he heard the sound of a heartbeat. The walls of the room seemed to close in on them. The stale air was stifling. Anubis must be near.

Every hair on his neck prickled. Across the room, Rachel's eyes were wide with fear.

"Ånp neb-Tatchesertt, bak n m netr netri. Ånp neb-Tatchesertt, bak n m netr netri!" General H. chanted. The mummies accompanied him. Their voices were dry and whispery, like autumn leaves blowing across an empty street.

The Scorpion King planted his golden spear in the dirt floor and lifted the canopic jar from the altar. The lid flipped up on a hinge, and the Scorpion King placed the jar under General H.'s chin. "The time has come," the Scorpion King roared.

Ungricht cried out gleefully, "Now, breathe out! Let your soul fill the jar, and Anubis will care for it well!"

General H. exhaled mightily, his nostrils flaring, but nothing happened.

The Scorpion King roared in anger.

"Don't hold back," Commandant R. warned from the side of the altar. "Don't you dare hold back, or they will kill us all!"

A heavy sweat broke out on General H.'s brow. He exhaled with renewed vigor and suddenly groaned in pain. He swayed on his knees, peering around with glazed eyes, but still he kept chanting.

A dark shape like a shadow began to form under his nose. At first Alex thought he only imagined it, but the shadow grew.

Something was coming out of his nostrils. Two black cobras!

Behind Rachel, even Commandant R. stiffened in fear. As General H. chanted, the snakes wiggled farther and farther, growing as long as whips. They flew around the room, twisting through the air like eels in water.

As General H. finished chanting, the snakes slithered through the fog into the canopic jars. The hinged lid closed with a snap, and the Scorpion King raised the jar high for all to see.

"Your soul is ours!" he roared triumphantly.

18

ANUBIS

"He comes!" Ungricht shouted. "Beware, he comes, the Lord of the Dead!"

All at once, the black fog around the altar drew together, taking form. Anubis spoke with a voice like a roaring earthquake. The words rumbled up into Alex's mind, and he found that he understood them perfectly.

"Bow to the Lord of the Dead, for I am your master now, and shall be through all eternity!"

Anubis was fifteen feet tall and towered over everyone—including the Scorpion King. He seemed like a giant with skin as gray as volcanic rock and a jackal's head. His strong arms and wrists were as thick as tree trunks and covered with warts. Hairs bristled from each wart. His white eyes glared. His jackal lips were curved into a snarl that displayed enormous fangs. Slobber ran down his chin. The monster stank of rotting flesh.

Commandant R. was paralyzed with fear and loosened his grip on Rachel's arm. She glanced quickly around the room again, searching.

Alex clutched the flare gun and tried to imagine shooting Anubis in the chest. *But will it do any good?* he wondered. He doubted that anything could hurt such a monster.

Anubis opened his palm and dangled an amulet—a golden ankh on a chain—in front of General H.'s face. General H. cried out and grabbed greedily for the necklace.

Anubis snarled with a voice like thunder and roared at General H. "Fool, to sell your soul so cheaply! For worlds on end, you shall regret your bargain, and all mankind will suffer with you!"

"Sieg Heil!" General H. shouted in reply. He grasped the chain, and the image of Anubis began to shimmer and fade. Small bolts of blue lightning shot through it, and Anubis was gone.

All of a sudden, Alex heard a snarl behind him, and a creepy voice growled, "Now I've got you, you slimy brat!"

Foot Rot was crawling rapidly toward him. The legless ghoul had been left far behind as General H. made his procession into the temple. Now the little monster grabbed Alex's ankle and screamed, "I caught him! I caught him!"

All around the room, the mummies and Germans turned to stare. Alex tried to kick the ghoul away as he drew his flare gun from the sack.

"Alex!" Rachel screamed. "Get out of here!" She lunged forward and threw her shoulder into General H. The big German staggered backward. Rachel kicked the canopic jar, shattering it. The black cobras rose from the broken jar and began flying through the air angrily, as if searching for a victim.

"Get back!" Ungricht shouted to Commandant R.

The Scorpion King roared in outrage, "Infidels!" He picked up his golden spear.

Alex drew his flare gun and aimed at the monster. But Foot Rot grabbed his wrist. "Give that to me!" the ghoul shouted, discharging the gun.

Whoosh! The flare shot over the Scorpion King in a ball of fire. It bounced off the far wall and hit the cobras in midair. They caught fire at once. Sparks shot everywhere. The flare bounced off the wall again, struck the ceiling, came back, and landed—*thud!*—right in the chest of a mummy.

"I'm gonna feed you to the dogs!" Foot Rot roared at Alex.

Alex groped in his sack for his slingshot and quickly pulled out something metal. But it was only his flashlight!

"Run!" Rachel yelled as she came bounding toward him from across the room.

The Scorpion King hurled his spear. It whizzed past Rachel's head and landed in the wall next to Alex.

Commandant R. shouted, "Now you die!" He raised his pistol and fired. Rachel fell to the floor as if the bullet had hit her.

"Rachel!" Alex cried. He stared at her in shock. Rachel groaned in pain, then leapt to her feet and took off running past him.

Maybe Commandant R. missed, Alex thought.

Alex wrenched the spear free from the wall and stabbed Foot Rot, pinning the little ghoul to the floor.

"Ah!" the ghoul screamed. "You stinking ball of camel snot! I'll get you!"

Smoke billowed everywhere, filling the room. The flaming cobras sizzled and hissed as they glided through the air. Dozens of mummies, dry as the desert sand, burst into flame.

"Halt!" Commandant R. shouted, firing his pistol at Rachel again.

Alex turned to see if she had been hit, but she'd already run into the empty corridor. Alex raced after her.

The Scorpion King let out a cry, shouting to his warriors, "Kill the infidels!"

Alex's heart hammered in his throat. He glanced back and saw the Scorpion King charging toward him. Alex strained every muscle trying to get more speed. He ran faster than he'd ever run before, but Rachel managed to scramble even faster. The Scorpion King was hot on his heels.

Alex picked up speed, whizzing past stalactites and torches. Ahead, some mummies were walking down the corridor, and Rachel slammed into them, knocking them aside.

"Keep going!" Alex cried.

"I'm trying!" she shouted back, her voice echoing through the temple.

They reached the first of the pillars, where the trail began to climb. Alex glanced back. The Scorpion King was right behind him and gaining! Alex couldn't run any faster.

"Now I've got you!" The monster grabbed Alex's heel with a giant claw and lifted him up, swinging him ten feet above the ground.

Alex whirled around to face the creature. Torchlight flickered on the Scorpion King's carapace, and he held his tail high. His deadly stinger was as long as a sword, and it oozed green poison.

19

A SOUND OF RISING BATTLE

Alex was caught. The Scorpion King held him upside down, swinging him like a pendulum high above the ground. He still had the bag with his slingshot, but for the moment he was trapped in the monster's grasp.

Alex could think of nothing to do. All he could picture were the Arabic prayers tattooed on Ardeth Bay's face and the dark black robes his friend wore.

"Ardeth Bay," he finally cried. "Where are you?"

The Scorpion King laughed cruelly. "The Medjai cannot help you now, young fool! You are in the Temple of Anubis, and you are mine."

In the distance, Alex heard the anguished roar of an Anubis warrior. Swords rang out, and a man shouted *Allah yisallihmak!* For Alex, there was no mistaking the sounds of a rising battle. The Medjai had arrived! He dared to hope that he'd survive.

"No!" the Scorpion King shouted in alarm. For a moment he gazed ahead, up the row of pillars toward the fallen warriors.

In that moment of distraction, Alex reached into his sack and grabbed the huge slingshot and a single ball bearing. He was still upside down. The bag dropped to the floor. He had only one shot, but he figured that it was all he would get. The Scorpion King's horrid face was only five feet away. Alex loaded his slingshot and pulled the rubber strips back so far that his arm ached.

"Hey," Alex shouted. "Where I come from, we squash bugs like you!"

Alex took his shot, just as the Scorpion King jerked away. The steel ball flew past the drooling creature and rolled to the floor.

"Aaargh!" he cried in anger. "Now there will be no mercy."

Alex closed his eyes tight and prepared for the end.

20

THROUGH STORM AND DARKNESS

The golden Spear of Osiris flew through the air and hit the Scorpion King right between the eyes. The monster's head snapped back from the force, and Alex dropped to the floor.

"Greetings, friend," a deep voice called out.

Alex rolled to his feet and looked up. The man's black robes were coated with sand, but Alex would recognize his face anywhere. "Ardeth Bay!" he cried. "I–I thought you'd never come. How did you get here just in time?"

"Only a desert storm could keep us from you—but not for long. We always come when we are needed. It is the way of the Medjai." Ardeth Bay smiled and looked across the room. The Scorpion King looked dead, but his huge tail quivered and lashed out, burying itself in a nearby pillar. "Now we must go," he said, "and save the stories for later."

From down in the inner temple, Alex heard shouting in German. General H. was screaming in outrage, *"Meine Seele! Meine Seele!"* A shot rang out, and a bullet whizzed over Ardeth Bay's head.

Commandant R. came rushing down the corridor, but the body of the Scorpion King blocked his way for a few moments.

Ardeth Bay grabbed Alex's hand, and together they ran down the corridor. As they ran, Alex searched for Rachel. "Please be all right," he whispered.

The barking of Anubis warriors became louder as they rounded the last corner. A dozen Medjai were at the temple door, swords flashing in the torchlight as they fought the jackal-headed warriors. "Alex!" they cried gratefully. "You are well!"

All around him, brave Medjai shouted war cries and fought with the strength of desperation. Hundreds of Anubis warriors surrounded the temple. The Medjai could not hold them off long.

Rachel was in the middle of them with the sword from a fallen Medjai. She raced fearlessly into battle, chopping the legs out from under one Anubis warrior and stabbing another in the heart.

"Rachel, you're alive!" Alex shouted in amazement.

"Not if we don't get out of here!" Rachel replied.

"Come, my friends!" Ardeth Bay called. "Let's go!"

The Medjai turned and raced into the storm. The blowing sand stung like flies. Alex raised his arm to protect his eyes. The storm had blown out all of the bonfires.

A flash of lightning struck. The light was a muddy brown, as if the sand were some sort of giant veil. In the glow he could see no landmarks at all, only strange mounds that had not been there before. He tripped in drifts of sand, following the Medjai.

Alex suddenly smacked into something big and fleshy. "An Anubis warrior!" he shouted in alarm.

Another flash of lightning split the sky, flickering like a serpent's tongue. The Medjai's laughter followed. It wasn't an Anubis warrior after all—only Stinkwad and the rest of the Medjai's camels. In relief, Rachel grabbed Stinkwad around the neck and patted him gently.

"Let's get out of here!" she shouted.

The Medjai were already mounting. Ardeth Bay was helping a wounded Arab onto his camel.

"Wait," Alex called to Rachel. "Aren't you bleeding?"

"Should I be?"

"You got shot! I saw it!" Alex knew that sometimes when people were hurt, they went into shock.

"The bullet just knocked me down," Rachel said. Alex stared at her in the darkness, confused, until Rachel raised her hand. Lightning flickered, and in its dull glow he saw a flash of gold. In her palm Rachel held the Ankh of Anubis. "Solid gold chains break easily," she explained. "You'd know that if you wore jewelry."

Alex let out a snort that was half surprise and half relief. So she *had* been shot. But the ankh protected her. So long as she held it, she could not be killed for a thousand years—and the Germans could be defeated. Their deal with the dead was over.

21

THE ESCAPE

Alex climbed onto his camel with Rachel, as the Medjai helped the wounded get mounted. An engine droned behind him. Alex turned and saw the plane's headlights come on. In the garish light, he watched the shadowy figures of General H., Commandant R., and Ungricht race up the ladder into the plane. Anubis warriors and mummies swarmed out of the temple.

The ground trembled, and the golden pyramid began to sink into the earth. A black cloud issued from its mouth, and the Scorpion King's face briefly appeared in that cloud.

With a voice louder than thunder, the Scorpion King roared in rage. "Infidels! There is no escape from death. There is no escape from Anubis! I shall have you yet!"

Instantly, the golden pyramid of Anubis disappeared from view. Not even the diamond that graced its tip could be seen.

Ardeth Bay climbed onto his camel.

"You hit him with the spear!" Alex cried. "I saw it. I thought he was dead!"

Ardeth Bay shook his head. "Some evils are so great that they never die. The Scorpion King is one of them. The most you can hope to do is drive him off for a while."

Ardeth Bay pointed to the plane in the distance. "I fear that Hitler is a real enemy, worse than any creature in the tombs. Every day he gains more power. Who knows what might happen . . ."

Alex nodded gravely and watched as his enemies turned their plane into the wind, the engines sputtering to life. The plane rumbled across the broken field, bouncing over piles of blowing sand. The wings dipped up and down, tossed by every current of air. Alex imagined that at any moment the plane would crash. But to his disappointment, it finally rose into the sky.

It rumbled out of the valley of Ahm Shere, past lightning bolts and clouds of sand, until its lights were lost from sight.

Alex wanted to be glad that he got out alive, but he still had a hollow feeling. They not only had escaped from the Scorpion King and stolen General H.'s soul, Rachel had gotten possession of the ankh. The Germans would not be able to rule for a thousand years. Yet Ardeth Bay was right. Alex's flare had not struck Ungricht or General H. or Commandant R. They had escaped.

He repeated to himself the words of Ardeth Bay, "Some evils are harder to destroy than others." They couldn't stop the Germans this time, but Ungricht was a tomb robber by profession. Alex suspected that they would meet again. *Next time,* Alex promised himself. *Next time, no escape.*

22

THE BRAVE MEDJAI

The Medjai took refuge a few miles from the temple, in the shelter of some rocks. An hour before dawn, the wind lost its fury, and the moon and stars began to shine.

The men sat around a campfire, drinking coffee. Ardeth Bay asked Rachel and Alex to tell the tale of their adventure with the Scorpion King.

"It was Alex's idea to fight them," Rachel started. She gave them details of what had happened, elaborating on Alex's fight with the mummy guards and journey into the temple. She made him sound so brave and powerful that Alex wondered if she was talking about someone else. He fell silent, embarrassed.

Ardeth Bay patted Alex on the back, then drew his curved dagger from its scabbard. The handle was made of gold and shaped like a lion, with rubies for eyes. The blade flashed gold in the firelight.

"This is ancient," Ardeth Bay told Alex. "It came down from my father and his father and his father before him. Saladin himself once bore this dagger. It has always been the dagger of a Medjai. Now it is yours. You are on your way to being a Medjai. Someday you will be a full protector of mankind."

Alex held the knife up and saw the horned moon reflected on its blade. He was overwhelmed and thrilled. "I will treasure it always."

"You have earned it many times over during this journey," Ardeth Bay answered. "But come, the storm is fading, and we must leave this evil place. Let us put some distance between ourselves and that cursed temple."

As they broke camp, Rachel took the ankh and, using Alex's knife, began to cut it in half.

"What are you doing?" Alex asked, worried. The ankh had kept Rachel alive when she might have been killed.

"I'm destroying it," Rachel said.

"But you could do a lot of good with something like that," he objected. "You should have seen how tough you looked, swinging a sword in the Temple of Anubis."

"And if I keep it," Rachel said, "what then? I may be strong, but stronger men will take it from me. The Germans might get it back, and all would be lost. This way, no one gets it. Not me, not them."

Rachel cut the soft metal, then bent the ankh until it broke in half. She scooped a hole in the sand and buried half of the ankh. The rest she put in her pocket. They rode their camels until sunrise, then she buried the second half.

It was the bravest thing Alex had ever seen anyone do.

23
FOND FAREWELLS

Three days later, Alex, Rachel, and Ardeth Bay rode their camels into Cairo. The city was a band of green along the Nile, with white buildings squatting among the palms. Behind them, the golden hills of sand stretched farther than the eye could see.

They reached Alex's house shortly after noon. His parents had just pulled up to the curb and were unloading suitcases from the trunk. Curiously, they seemed to only have about half the suitcases that they had taken to England.

"Surprise! We're home!" his mum shouted when she saw Alex. She looked at the camels. "Have you two been out for a ride?"

"A short one," Ardeth Bay said with a sly grin.

"Everything's all right, I hope," Alex's mum said. "I did nothing but worry about you the whole trip."

"Everything's great," Alex said. He got down from the camel and hugged her.

"Thank you, Ardeth Bay. Our son looks fine," she said.

Alex's dad pulled the last of the suitcases from the trunk and teased, "See, I told you he'd be okay. I was just worried Alex would get bored to death."

Ardeth Bay laughed. "You underestimate me, O'Connell. Have you forgotten our two adventures together?"

Alex's father smiled. "How could I? Rotted mummies, cursed skeletons—" his eyes narrowed. "You and Alex didn't get in any trouble, did you?"

"Dad," Alex sighed.

"Of course not, friend," Ardeth Bay replied. He winked at Alex.

Alex's mum squeezed him again, then took his hands and stared into his eyes. "I can't wait another minute, so I'll tell you now. Guess what? I have such good news. The scholars at Bembridge loved the speech I delivered. They've asked me to move back to London. I'm going to teach!"

"You're moving back to London?" Alex asked.

She grinned. "No, *we're* moving back to London, silly!"

"But—when?" Alex asked.

"As soon as we get packed," his dad said. "The school term starts next week."

Alex stared in surprise.

His mum said, "I know that it's all rather sudden. I haven't even had time to get used to the idea myself!"

"It'll be great," Alex's dad said, ruffling Alex's hair. "Don't worry. Ardeth Bay will visit us, right?"

Ardeth Bay nodded. "Just as soon as I can. Now let me say goodbye to Alex, then I'll join you and Evelyn inside."

"All right." Alex's parents picked up their luggage and headed for the house.

Alex looked up at Ardeth Bay, who still sat on his camel. "I guess this means that I can't be a Medjai after all. I should give your knife back."

Ardeth Bay merely smiled. "Keep it. You are training to be a Medjai, and the Medjai are protectors of mankind. You can become a Medjai in London as well. Besides, my heart tells me that you will return. Your mother is a student of Egypt, and your father is an adventurer. They've saved the world from mummies twice before. And now you have, too. They will come back with you, you'll see."

Someday, Alex thought. He didn't want to live anywhere but Egypt.

He looked up at Rachel on Stinkwad. Rachel's eyes were glistening with tears. He thought of her as a friend, a new friend. Yet in some ways, he felt closer to her than anyone he knew.

"I'll come back someday," he said. "Will you and your father be here?"

"As long as Hitler remains in Germany, our home is in Egypt," Rachel replied.

"What if the Germans find you?" Alex asked nervously.

"Then I will call my new friends the Medjai . . . and if they don't come, I will fight as bravely as you."

Alex smiled. "Will you take care of Stinkwad for me? I know he smells bad—"

"You think he smells bad?" Rachel said. "How could he smell bad. He's the fastest-running, best mummy-killing camel in all Egypt. I think he smells wonderful."

She bit her lip.

Alex took her hands and squeezed them. He was turning to go when Rachel bent down and gave him a piece of crumbling stone from the Scorpion King's temple.

"To remember me—and Egypt," she whispered. "Thank you, for everything. Don't worry about Stinkwad. We'll both be here the next time you're ready for an adventure."

ABOUT ANCIENT EGYPT

THE EGYPTIANS

More than 5,000 years ago, Egypt was ruled by kings who were thought to be so powerful, they were believed to be direct descendants of the sun god Re. Ancient Egyptians called their rulers *pharaohs* and built great tombs, called pyramids, to honor them. They also developed a sophisticated and highly effective method of preserving their pharaohs' bodies after death, a process known as mummification.

THE PYRAMIDS

• A pyramid is a huge stone structure with a rectangular base and four sloping triangular sides that usually meet at a point. They were meant to help pharaohs make a successful journey to the afterlife.

• There are more than 180 pyramids spread out over Egypt and the Sudan (in northern Africa). All the pyramids in Egypt are on the west bank of the Nile River, which was believed to be the home of the setting sun and the resting place of the sun god, Re.

• The most famous are the three large pyramids at Giza, outside Egypt's capital city, Cairo. The Great Pyramid of King Khufu, in Giza, is the largest pyramid still standing. It was the tallest structure in existence until the Eiffel Tower was finished in 1889. In its original condition, the Great Pyramid was 481 feet tall, and its base was 756 feet long on each side. It is composed of more than 2,250,000 stones, each weighing approximately 5,000 pounds. The blocks are placed so firmly together that a credit card won't fit between them.

• There are no records to tell us how pyramids were built. Ancient accounts claim it took 100,000 men 20 years to complete the Great Pyramid at Giza. It probably took 4,000 men a full year. Most likely, teams of Egyptians pulled the heavy stones and bricks on a sled up a ramp, which was built up as the pyramid rose. Unfortunately, much of the fine limestone that once formed a smooth cover on the outside of the pyramids was later removed and used to construct buildings throughout Egypt.

• Since the pyramids were intended to be sacred, everlasting tombs for great gods, they were designed to house the mummy in complete safety. The actual tombs were buried deep in the heart of the pyramid. The rest of the pyramid was designed to deter would-be robbers with features like dead-end passageways, mazelike corridors, false doors with carved hinges, 50-ton stone slabs blocking doorways, and false burial chambers. Despite these efforts, most pyramids were completely looted before 1000 B.C.

THE SPHINX

• The Sphinx is a mythical creature with a lion's body and a pharaoh's head. A huge sculpture of the sphinx is poised outside Khafra's pyramid at Giza and was probably meant to guard the king's tomb. The colossal figure is one of the most famous monuments in Egypt.

• The Sphinx is more than 65 feet tall and 185 feet long. It was carved from limestone and faces east, toward the rising sun, the symbol of rebirth and renewal.

• During the past 4,500 years, violent and long-lasting sandstorms covered the Sphinx in sand all the way up to its neck. The sand actually had a preservative, protective effect. Unfortunately, the statue has been suffering from the corrosive effects of pollution since the sand was cleared away in 1925.

MUMMIES

• Mummification preserves a body by removing moisture and preventing the growth of bacteria that cause the flesh to decay. The Egyptians believed that the soul would meet the body in the afterlife, so bodies needed to be well preserved and highly recognizable. The earliest Egyptian mummies date from 3200 B.C.

To mummify a body, the Egyptians:

1. Removed the brain through the nose, using a small, hooklike instrument.
2. Made a small incision in the abdomen and removed the major organs, except for the heart. They believed the mummy would need the heart for passage into the afterlife.
3. Mummified the organs separately and placed them in small, beautiful urns called canopic jars.
4. Cleansed the skin with oils, herbs, and wine.
5. Applied more than 40 pounds of natron, a form of salt, for 30 to 50 days to dry the body.
6. Applied generous amounts of oils, wax, and resins (tree sap) to make the skin more supple and lifelike.
7. Filled the body cavity with sand, linen, or even peppercorns to preserve its shape.
8. Applied layers of shrouds and hundreds of yards of linen bandages, a process that took almost 15 days.

9. After the body was prepared, its head was covered with a mask made of gold or plaster, and an apron was placed over its torso.

10. Bandaged mummies were then placed in a wooden coffin. The case was meant to protect the mummy from tomb robbers and house the dead person's spirit. Mummy masks and coffins were richly decorated with symbols and hieroglyphics (picture writing) containing spells and tips for ensuring eternal life.

11. Mummies were entombed with everything they could possibly need in the afterlife, including food, jars, furniture, tools, jewelry, slippers, makeup, bread, toys, mirrors, musical instruments, and even games.

ABOUT THE AUTHOR

Dave Wolverton is a *New York Times* bestselling author with thirty-five books to his credit. He has written more than a dozen books for middle-grade readers set in the Star Wars universe, including the Jedi Apprentice series. He set a new Guinness record for the world's largest book signing on July 3, 1999.

Besides writing books, he has helped design such bestselling video games as StarCraft's Broodwar and Xena: The Talisman of Fate for Nintendo 64, and Runelords for Gameboy. He is currently producing his first short film and teaches science fiction and fantasy writing at Brigham Young University in Provo, Utah.

Dave Wolverton can be reached by e-mail at dwolvert@itsnet.com.

The Evolution of Adventure Continues . . .

Relive the excitement of the film with the official movie tie-in books—including the *Jurassic Park™ III Movie Storybook* plus the earth-shattering new Jurassic Park™ Adventures series!

A Totally New and Exciting Way to Learn About Dinosaurs!

www.jpinstitute.com

Available June 12, 2001, wherever books are sold.

www.randomhouse.com/kids

© 2001 Universal Studios Publishing Rights, a division of Universal Studios Licensing, Inc. Jurassic Park is a trademark and copyright of Universal Studios and Amblin Entertainment, Inc. All Rights Reserved.

BFYR274